The
SOUND

Published with support from the
Fremantle Press Champions of Literature

First published 2016 by
FREMANTLE PRESS
25 Quarry Street, Fremantle WA 6160
www.fremantlepress.com.au

Editor Georgia Richter
Cover design Carolyn Brown
Cover photograph Sergey Sizov, www.shutterstock.com
Printed by Everbest Printing Company, China

National Library of Australia
Cataloguing-in-Publication entry:

Drummond, Sarah, 1970–
The sound / Sarah Drummond
ISBN: 9781925163759
Sealers (persons) — Western Australia — History — Fiction
Women, Aboriginal Australian — Western Australia — History — Fiction
First contact with Europeans— Western Australia — Fiction
Dewey Number: A823

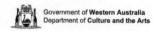

Fremantle Press is supported by the State Government through the Department of Culture and the Arts. Publication of this title was assisted by the Commonwealth Government through the Australia Council, its arts funding and advisory body.

The SOUND

A NOVEL BY
SARAH DRUMMOND

 FREMANTLE PRESS

For my mum, Carmelita O'Sullivan

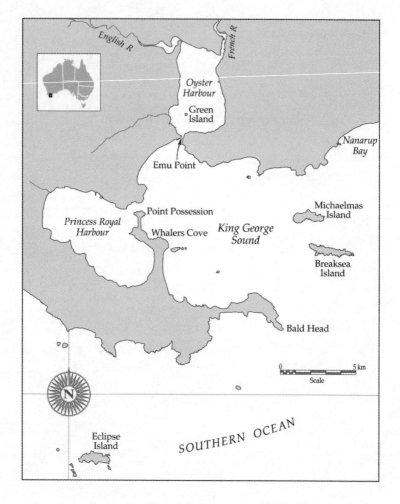

KING GEORGE SOUND, WESTERN AUSTRALIA, 1827.

King George Sound January 1827

My name is Wiremu Heke. Some people call me Billhook. On this day, with the story I had to tell, the Major called me Mister Hook. I stood outside a canvas tent on a reedy foreshore in the cleavage of two mountains, from which grey plates of granite channelled water down to the inlet. There were no buildings here, no roads or even horses, only a few tents, the bush and a brig sitting out on the water. I was oceans away from my home and I was waiting to be interviewed about a murder.

Beside me a soldier jingled the keys to my handcuffs. My stomach felt sharp and tight. Golden light filtered through the tent, musty from the ship's hold. I stood at the flap, looking in. A young man stared out at me, like a child who has heard stories of savages and cannibals. Only his white man's stiffness stopped him from reaching out to touch the pounamu stretching my earlobe, or the huge, glossy teeth around my neck. The young man sniffed and touched his nostrils with soft fingers. From the set of his eyes and his jaw, he must have been the son of the man writing at the desk behind him.

"Sir," the soldier said. "William Hook, sir."

The Major twisted in his chair and I looked down to the frayed canvas feathering my feet. The Major had just shaved and his jowls gleamed. He stood, a straight man.

"Are you from the same gang as Samuel Bailey?"

"*Gov'nor Brisbane* sir, yes."

"Where are you from, Mister Hook?"

From the little bay, where the eels are, near the marae, before the sand spit, before the open cliffs where the kelp surges like great black snakes in the swell.

"Aramoana. Otakau."

"A native of the south island of New Zealand." He sat and wrote. "Māori." His hand stayed on the paper and he looked at me. "The *Sophia*?"

Ae, they all know, these men under the banner of the King. They know who did the burning and the killing. My father on the beach, bleeding, his fleet of waka sawn in half by Kelly and his thugs. But those men don't know the smell of my charred Otakau. The work of a torch and a following wind.

The Major's grim smile made me want to turn and leave his stinking golden tent but there was the idling soldier, and there were things that I needed done.

"I was a boy sir."

"Approximately twenty years of age." The Major wrote on his paper again. He asked me questions and then the same questions again. He ran around my story of the killing and then around it again. The Major wrote all of the names down carefully. His son returned with sweet black tea in white cups and the tent grew warmer with its steam and our bodies and the climbing sun. Finally the Major dipped the end of a pen in ink, blotted it on rough paper and handed it to me.

"Sign please."

I stared at the black lines tattooing the paper. "If I do this, then you will go to the island and rescue Tama Hine and Moennan."

The Major sighed. "Your ... sort are called sea wolves and pirates and that is in polite society, Mister Hook. Worse down on the docks. Your crimes in King George Sound have created tremendous hardship for my men and myself. Your actions are –"

"I beg your pardon, sir. But will you get them from the island?"

"My pardon is the least of your concerns." But he nodded. "First light. I intend to have Samuel Bailey arrested."

I bent over the table and signed the paper.

X.

Aramoana 1825

Wiremu Heke was newly a man when the chiefs called a public meeting about Captain Kelly and the *Sophia*. Wiremu's father limped along. He was too broken to work but the elders held him in high esteem. Eight years after the attack and the people still wanted revenge. Several young men needed to avenge fathers and mothers who had died from the bullets. It was part of their heritage and their right, they argued, to gather up honour, the way the white man gathers up medals and stripes.

They had to find the sea captain. For all the rumours and stories from visiting whalers, Kelly and the *Sophia* never returned to Whareakeake or Murdering Bay as the whalers called it. Wiremu's father knew of his son's hankerings and volunteered him to the sea and a seaman's life in search of information on the Captain's whereabouts. "Send young Wiremu. He is hungry for the ocean." Wiremu was hungry for the girl Kiri too but the sea collected him up like a cuttlebone.

The chiefs ordered him and five other young men to work aboard the whalers, to collect crop seeds and knowledge from the shores of New South Wales, and find Captain Kelly. If they found him, they would entice him to return on a peace mission to Otakau where the chiefs would be waiting for him. No man explained to Wiremu how to garner a sea captain.

Life for this Otakau boy changed quickly after the meeting. A sealing schooner arrived and its captain offered to take him aboard as a mate to Van Diemen's Land, where he could then work his way to the New South Wales colony. He had time to romance the girl but briefly, in a sweaty rush by the river. She had a knowing glint in her eye that he would leave soon. Kiri's breath whistled as she cried out, and later as she slept on the thatch mat he'd laid down for her, he watched her breathe. When she awoke, he asked her about her wheeze. She did not think of herself as unhealthy or ill. "Born on the river, Wiremu," she said, stroking his face. "Born on the river."

His father arranged for Wiremu to be tattooed. He squatted on the mat beside his son and talked as the tattooist worked. His father told him stories to distract him from the pain of the chisel. He talked and talked. It seemed rudderless talk until Wiremu realised he was talking his way into ancestral stories, carving them into Wiremu's memory while the tattooist carved the spirals into his flesh.

He told Wiremu how he came to build boats, the same boats Wiremu would paddle out beyond the heads to catch barracouta. He had learned his trade from his uncle who had learned from his grandfather. Wiremu's great-grandfather was first a boatbuilder, but when he was broken by his enemy's mere, he became a carver of wood and then a tohunga tā kaue, a carver of flesh.

Wiremu's great-grandfather had fallen in love with a Ngai Tahu girl. She was the daughter of a visiting chief. She wore a necklace of orca teeth. She saw Wiremu's great-grandfather carving into bartered kauri, on the edge of the river where he lived with his wife and son. She watched him carve the ocean into the wood with chisel and hammer. He may well have been using a leaf, his blows and strokes were so fine. He asked the wood politely to work for him. She saw that and she asked him, "Why don't you work it harder and it will be quicker?" He replied that he must ask or the ocean would be lost. It was a mere he was carving and as he smoothed his hand over the wood, he thought that one day it may kill a man or break him, and his blood would fall over the earth like resin. Only when she said she had sought him out because she was told he could give her moko, did he look up at the girl.

"Ae," Wiremu's father sighed and smiled.

The next day Wiremu's great-grandfather laid her down on reed matting in a cool shelter. She turned up her chin to him and he gripped it in his hard carver's hands. She was sweating. He gave her narcotic seeds to chew and told her to leave the pulp under her tongue so the juices would spread to the back of her mouth. It made her saliva rise and she was soon light-headed.

He stirred the liquid in the bowl beside him, the ash of burnt shit and fish oil, water. He laid out the contents of his tool bag: a handle of manuka and blades made from the wings of albatrosses, some with serrated edges and some flat and sharp. He wound the handle to the blade with string. Then he began to carve her, tapping the bone blade against her face with a small wooden mallet.

He carved for most of the day, rubbing his black concoction into her wounds, wiping away her spills of blood with a softened flax cloth. At first the pain was unbearable but her flesh was soon numb with the drug and the hammering. The sound of the chisel thudded against her skull, eased by his voice as he told her stories of his ancestors.

One of the kuia, her grandmother, helped her to her feet and they left the shelter. She could not open her mouth for three days. She felt unable to breathe. She could not eat. Her belly an empty hut. Her grandmother had moko. Now very old, she sat with blankets around her shoulders and knees. When she spoke, she pointed out the girl with lips long ago blackened by the ink of burned caterpillars and tree resin, and it was like an accusation when she told her she was under the spell of the tohunga tā kaue. She liked to smoke a pipe, though she told her granddaughter never to do this. She also instructed her not to eat fatty foods or embrace a man until her moko was healed. If she did these things, the black lines would bleed and disappear and she would be forever shamed as a woman who had disrespected her moko.

She stayed in the hut, hiding her swollen face. On the fourth day she emerged to see the tattooist being chased from his hut by an angry woman wielding a stick. After the kui had given her leaves to protect her lips, she went to see her father. He told her off for taking moko without asking his permission but she was ready for womanhood and quietly he was pleased, she knew. She asked him about the tohunga tā kaue.

They married, the girl with the orca tooth necklace and the carver of wood and flesh. Together they travelled around the island. He tattooed many other people. His tattoos always depicted the sea, the waves and the spirals of the spirits that eddied in the shallows. Everyone who saw Wiremu Heke's great-grandfather's moko recognised his work.

Wiremu's father talked all day. He gave him all of his stories the day before Wiremu sailed out of Otakau with tender, freshly tattooed buttocks, to cross the sea to Van Diemen's Land.

HOBART 1825

"Go west. Go west!" The man who leaned into Wiremu's face had piano-peg teeth. "Boss Davidson doesn't mind playing his chances. We'll make a good lay from the sealskin and be out of the way of the Governor and King. Not a white man to be seen in the west." Seal were getting fished out of the Strait, he said. Seal were getting scarce and the Islanders controlled their patch with firearms. A good time to go west.

It was a tavern at the Hobart docks, where men heaved and swayed like the sea inside the sandstone walls. Samuel Bailey gave Wiremu another mug of wine and spoke to the red-faced man who was his boss. "His name is Billhook. Easier to say than his real name. Billhook will do. He's a real good blackfella. Take him on, eh?"

All the sweat, the people so close, the wine and then Boss Davidson's offer; it was as confusing as it was intoxicating. Wiremu, christened Billhook by his crewmates, stood on the docks the next day and watched the *Governor Brisbane* shifting against the pylons.

Not north to New South Wales for Billhook. He shipped out of Hobart Town three days later bound for the west country. Men crawled amongst the rigging like possums in trees. It took them another three days along the Derwent and through Storm Bay to get to the sea. They were becalmed in the mornings, drifting under hills made smoky blue by the mist, and then away as the midday wind worked up the water writhing black with the shining spines of humpback whales.

During the three days, Billhook began to know the crew. It was said that Samuel Bailey was a swell's son run out. He was wind-burned, with deep cracks around his mouth. A white man. Billhook quickly realised he would never know the weather coming with Bailey. His eyes clouded all the storms in his heart until the moment he lashed out. He got wild alright but Bailey getting wild made him steady as a snake.

Pigeon was a black man, a Sydney native, who quickly got on side with Boss Davidson with his clever wit, and his great strength which belied his lanky frame. A boy called Neddy, born on Kangaroo Island to a black woman and a sealer there. The brothers Jack and Tommy Blunt were the first white men Billhook had met who were born in this country. Two black men: Black Simon towered over Billhook, his back ribbed with scars of the lash, he spoke with a strange accent; and Hamilton, a small, very dark man with an easy smile who could speak many languages. Jimmy was the crew's boatsteerer. The men called him Jimmy the Nail because he had once driven a pike through a rival's hand and nailed him to the starboard gunwale of his whaleboat. He was a short, sandy man with a ready humour and a scar down the side of his nose. Pigeon told Billhook that Jimmy the Nail had shot black men at their fires to get women. Pigeon knew this because he'd helped him find their camps at night.

At Robbins Island on the western fringes of the Strait, they weighed anchor and went ashore to gather more crew and supplies for the journey west. Boss Davidson and Jimmy the Nail haggled for pork, sealskins and women with a bluff sealer, who introduced himself as the Strait's Policeman.

The first time Billhook saw Vandiemonian women, they were returning to the hut from muttonbirding, long sharp sticks slung across their shoulders, threaded with fluffy grey chicks. Seven women. One child. Twenty dogs. Big dogs they were, some as high as the women's waists. Long-legged hunting curs, all lolling tongues and ears askew and whiskery grins.

The women walked over the bald hill towards the hut, spread out in a line, the sun behind them, so that their dark shapes with the sticks looked like the white man's martyr. Some of the impaled birds flapped wearily in the wind as though still alive. The wind tossed the island grass like an ocean about their legs. If the dogs hadn't been moving, their shaggy brindle pelts would have made them near invisible against the grass.

Billhook watched the women walk towards them.

Bailey muttered, "Which one do you want?"

"We got plenty pork," said Billhook and realised his mistake when Bailey laughed and pointed to the woman on the far right.

"That one."

She was short and strong and wore a frock of skins with the fur on the inside and a red knit cap. She was laughing but she stopped when she saw Bailey point her out. The clanswomen walked wide of the two men and cast down their eyes. They looked angry or shamed and not as strong as they did on the hill. Billhook's mother had made his sisters smear their faces with stinking dirt and messed their glossy hair with manure, when the white whalers first came to Aramoana. His sisters were only little girls then but his mother knew to keep them safe.

Bailey stood looking at the woman, chewing tobacco and spitting. His mouth moved around his screw jaw as if it hurt to speak. He took off his cap. He was not an old man but his hair ran away from his head, thin, soft wisps over pink skin.

From the highest point of the island Billhook could see a

conical hill on the coast of Van Diemen's Land. In the evening, a single line of smoke bloomed from the top.

"See that smoke?" he asked the Policeman. "On top of the mountain over there."

"It's the blackfellas," said the Policeman. "The fellas. That's why the Worthies light a fire up here too." He gestured behind him to the dark shapes of the women laying swathes of green branches over a frugal flame. A quick burst of smoke floated into the sky. "They're saying hello back to their fellas. Hello. Goodnight. Whatever they say."

"Worthies?"

"Titters. Tyreelore. Island Wives. Worth their weight, Billhook. We'd starve without 'em, hear me."

The women worked hard in the sea and on the land, the Policeman said. Scraping skins, collecting salt, hunting tammar and giving succour to men who smelt like muttonbird and seal. He talked of muttonbirding. The women went out to the muttonbird grounds with their dogs, spent the day putting their arms down burrows until their faces touched the ground. They showed the Straitsmen how to do this when they were first taken to the islands. Crouch down and thrust your arm into the hole after the parent birds had gone out hunting for fish. Crouch down until the grass and stones scratched your cheek. Feel the wriggle, the bleating heart of the fluffy chick, its feeble pecking at your hand, haul it out, break its neck over a stick, leave it on the ground for one of the other women to thread onto a stick before the dogs got to it. The worst job was draining the oil from the muttonbirds after they were plucked, and squeezing out the gurry. And the black snakes in the muttonbird burrows. Snakes everywhere. Lurking in the bushes they called barking barillas. Full of snakes after baby chicks and eggs. But no one ever seemed to get bitten by the snakes. Sometimes they felt the dry slither of a tail but if snake felt you coming they left you alone.

"You hunt and clean muttonbirds too?"

"Nah," said the Policeman. "That's the Worthies' job. That woman Mary," the Policeman pointed to one of the women. "She's the wallaby woman. She's got six dogs. Between all the women there be twenty-eight dogs so they're a job to feed. Fine dogs they are. Quick and quiet. Like the lurchers from the old country. Their husbands steal them from the shepherds over on the mainland, or trade them and breed them up. Good hunters they are. Never rush a mob of kangaroo without knowing which one they want. Twenty roo in one day once and the Worthies had their skins pegged out by dinnertime. She's good with dogs, that Mary, but she's gettin' difficult. I reckon she'll be aboard with you lot."

The Policeman sold Boss Davidson two women, Dancer and Mary, to take west aboard the *Governor Brisbane*. The strong one, the woman Bailey had pointed out to Billhook, the Policeman wanted to keep her. He was attached to her, he said. He fingered the hard edges of the sealskins that Jimmy had traded him for Dancer. Behind him, a girl child of about eight peered around the doorway and spoke to Mary in her native language. The Policeman turned and spat, "Git!" and she snapped her head out of sight.

In the morning Boss sent his crew in to the island. On the shore, Dancer and Mary waited until the pigs were dumped in the bottom of the dinghy and then climbed aboard and sat on the warm carcasses. Mary turned her face away from the island and from her dogs, which milled about the shoreline, crying for her.

The *Governor Brisbane* shipped out midmorning. Billhook looked down from his spar in alarm as Dancer began to wail loudly. She and Mary sat huddled on the foredeck, Dancer's face greying as the swell rose. She cried out in her language and threw up. Boss Davidson, standing at the wheel, grinned at her and shook his head.

"You must have a padlock on yer arse, Dancer, shitting through yer teeth like that."

"The water makes her sick," said Mary and stroked Dancer's short cap of hair. She took her amulet pouch and sprinkled something powdery and red into Dancer's outstretched palm. Then she held the pouch against Dancer's belly and spoke in swift, watery language. "And there's Devil in this sea 'ere," she called to Boss Davidson, and Boss nodded like he knew what she was saying.

Mary was right. Currents sucked away from sandbars and surged into strange whirlpools. Westerly winds crashed into the easterly swell, complicating the backwash from the rocky cliffs. It was a glad feeling to be away from the islands and into the open sea, away from those uncanny surges, to see the islands sink away and become a mere smudge on the horizon, the sea glittering with an aslant sun and deep blue, rising up to meet the schooner. Dancer quit her crying and vomiting when the islands were out of sight.

They butchered the two pigs on the first afternoon and salted the pork into barrels. They used most of the salt aboard as Boss had plans to get more at Kangaroo Island.

"There's a few tars there too, who'll want a lay," he said that evening.

Kangaroo Island came up on the horizon on the morning of the fourth day. The island rose out of the sea like a beast in the heat's magic haze. They sailed through the Backstairs Passage, where Jimmy the Nail, who'd lived there, told Billhook that a woman had escaped her island captors by swimming seventeen miles back to the mainland. "With a baby strapped to her back." They sailed past the cliffs of the cape and into Newland Bay. Billhook, Bailey and Jimmy the Nail rowed the dinghy towards a white shore, the boat swishing over seagrass beds, the water flattened by the lee of the island. It began to rain softly.

Three men and a woman ran down the rocky hill to where the boat rocked in the shallows. Dogs yapped around their legs. Two more black women dressed in wallaby smocks and knit caps dragged sacks of salt along the beach. One of the women smoked a pipe as she worked.

"See those tars?" Jimmy the Nail pointed to the men gathered on the beach to watch them wade ashore. "See their uniforms? Those ones still wearin' slops. By the time they been here five years they'll be in skins like the blackfellas and will have some say in matters. Now see that bloke. That's Jim Kirby. He bin here a while."

Kirby was red-faced with hair once orange and now faded to a bright yellow. His long beard was red and white. He was dressed in skins which he couldn't have cured too well for they smelled bad and rotted off his body, falling into tatters about his knees.

"And this is Smidmore," Jimmy muttered to Billhook. "Me old mate."

Smidmore was dark but no native. A Gael perhaps or one of the Black Irish with spiralling black hair that he tied behind his neck with a leather thong and an eye that turned. He carried a fiddle, like the one played in the Hobart tavern, a gear sack and a gun. Smidmore hadn't been on the island long, from what Jimmy had told Billhook, for he wore the canvas slops given to all new sealers. Despite his clothing, Smidmore acted with Kirby as if they were lords of the island. Billhook wondered aloud to Jimmy why they would take on a lay as tars when they could be island chiefs. Jimmy replied quietly that they were being run off since Johnny Randall planned to go west too. And something about women. There had been some trouble with the women.

They loaded the little boat with two guns wrapped in oiled cloth, two bags of cabbages and potatoes and fifteen sacks of salt sewn closed with the sinew of kangaroo tails. One of the women climbed in, calling her two dogs after her. Kirby and Smidmore got in too. The men and women left on shore pushed out the boat until they felt it free from the sand. Bailey and Billhook grabbed at the oars. The women waved and sobbed and called to the woman in the boat. They rowed out to the channel that would take them through the breakers.

The black woman stood at the bow holding a rope, her feet planted firmly on the thwart. She was magnificent and when he could, Billhook turned to look at her. She looked different to the two Vandiemonian Worthies. Her face was thinner, her hair straighter and she didn't have strings of tiny shining shells about her throat. Instead, so tightly thonged that it dug into the hollow between her collarbones, she wore the whitened skull of a newborn baby.

The crew wriggled the boat alongside the *Governor Brisbane*. The wind had come up in the absence and it blew the boat off before anyone could get a rope. Hands grabbed for flying ropes on the next try and they fastened the dinghy. The island woman pointed to the salt and let Samuel Bailey know in good English that she'd collected it herself and it must be looked after. She had Bailey on the edge of nodding in obedience until he grunted and turned away.

Mary scowled at her from the schooner's deck. Mary had been boss woman on Robbins and Billhook could almost hear her thoughts. Who was this uppity sprite? And how was she allowed to bring her dogs and Mary not?

The woman threw one of her dogs up to the ship. The short,

whiskery terrier landed on deck and turned to snarl at Hamilton, the black jack, then looked over the side at his owner, wagging his tail. On her next throw the bigger dog, a lean hunting dog similar to Mary's, hit the stringers and dropped, shrieking, into the sea. She let out a cry of dismay. Bailey laughed. The dog swam around the dinghy, shaking water out of its ears. She hauled it in by the skin of its neck. The islander Smidmore grabbed a rope dangling from the gunwales and she tied it around the dog. She nodded to the black jack who hauled the animal up, its body hanging from its elbows, tail between its legs and looking down at its mistress with wrinkled brow.

Once her dogs were safely on board, she nodded again at the sacks of salt. "Don't you drop that salt. Plenty hard work," she said to Billhook. She looked at him hard. "You no white man." She pointed a good true east with long fingers. "You from over there?"

Billhook nodded.

"K'ora!" she said grinning, her teeth as white as her infant child's skull and Billhook grinned back in spite of himself.

Rope ladders tumbled down. He watched her climb and wondered how many rope ladders she'd climbed in the cover of night to see a white captain moored at the mouth of American River, a man who scribbled in his books about timber and soil and wallabies and winds but never of the black girl who climbed onto his ship and was shown to his cabin.

"Sal," said Smidmore to the men in the dinghy who were watching Sal climb aboard. "That's my Sal. She's mine."

Kangaroo Island to Israelite Bay 1825

The days were much the same until the storm hit. Wind blew over the starboard shoulder in the mornings and port side in the afternoons as the land warmed up and sucked the air in from the south. They rarely saw land and when they did, it was only to find anchorage. Then the land was a thin shabby strip misted and hazy with the afternoon salt spray.

Ten days into the journey across the Southern Ocean, the sky became a frightening greasy yellow, with fleeing petrels and tiny spotted clouds heralding the storm. At midnight Boss Davidson ordered the sails shortened. By dawn the *Governor Brisbane* was running under bare poles at ten knots, sideways. She careened towards the coast, slapping against whitecaps and lurching into valleys of sea. Boss ordered up the main, to get some reach.

For three days without sleep the crew fought to keep her off the red cliffs, where the country looked broken off and dropped into the sea. None of the men knew the colour of the sky during those days and nights, only the light on dark and heaving water. The cliffs stayed a smudge on the horizon, always present but no one wanted to look any closer.

The beach near the island was a shock of white sand after the long days of red cliffs. It was near here that one of Flinders' men met his maker, Boss Davidson said on the quiet morning after the storm. But not to worry of dead men. The Blunt brothers were to stay and get their lot of seal here. Elephant seal were fished out of the Strait and there was some oil money to be made.

Jack and Tommy were born in this country. Tommy had said that when they were babies the colony was starving because no one knew how to live there and they depended on ships for supplies. They grew all the wrong vegetables and the sheep and cattle ran off into the bush where they ate poisonous plants or were speared by blackfellas. When their mother's milk ran out, Tommy said, he became sick from dirty water and almost died. Lucky they were, Tommy said, with both parents sent out on the hulks, to be born free men. Jack said he just remembered being hungry.

Jack had the build of a coursing dog, all sinew and bone. He shaved his head every other day and wrapped a cloth around his skull. His eyes were thin. Wrinkles rippled around his lashes. Jack talked fast like gunshots, hard and sharp. He moved quick too and worked in bursts of speed. When Jack wasn't talking his silence was as hard as his words. His silence was like the stillness of a bad sky. Jack held his rage, nursed it like drink.

He tattooed himself all over his forearms; one was of a seal with the breasts and head of a woman, with no arms and bound in rope. In the nights after leaving Bass Strait, he'd pricked an image of the *Governor Brisbane* into his skin. He tattooed the ship so that when he stood, the ship was upside down with the roiling sea above her keel and her sails blooming towards the real sea. For the crew it was too bad an omen to look at without shaking their heads.

Jack talked about his twin brother: his carelessness, his untidiness or his clumsy feet. Tommy never seemed to notice the injury he caused Jack. Tommy not bothering to clear the gun. Tommy leaving the embers of a fire all wrong and out of place. Jack seethed with small hurts. When they split in their mother's womb it was like they'd been cut away from one another. Tommy had long hair that he never tied back. Shanks of it were always across his face. He never wore shoes or a hat. His feet were furry, his eyes wide and brown. Tommy had landed in a gentler, softer place than Jack, where he was never blown sideways in a gust, never narrowed his eyes against the midday glare, nor picked the gun stock's splinters from his skull after a beating. His legs were short and he was strong. His hands and wrists were chunky with muscle. He moved slowly but he got the work done. He was clever with boats and could spot a riff on the water long before it hit the sail.

The two young men were given knives, a gun, a water barrel, empty oil barrels, rations of salt pork and cabbages and one of the dinghies. At the cove, a small island broke the back of the open ocean and was supposed to be comfortable living. Boss Davidson cautioned the Blunt brothers to make their hut on the island as the natives in the area liked the white man a little too much.

"Weren't far from here that the *Aida* foundered and the last man to survive told of cannibals who came down from the desert and found his shipmates dying of thirst on the beach. And then they had worse things than dying of thirst to think about, you mark my words. He was raving, mind, when they found him. Worse than Billhook's mob, the blackfellas around here. You'll know the beach they washed up on when you find their oars stuck in the sand. Five oars standing up like saplings. Five oars."

Jack and Tommy's eyes flared at this. "I'm not gettin' eaten by no blackfella," said Jack. "You'd better be givin' us more powder than what we got."

As the little boat was lowered past the planks of the *Governor Brisbane*, Tommy looked up to Boss Davidson. "You be sure to return for us," he shouted. He looked afraid.

"Four months," said Boss Davidson. "You be gettin' those seal for me."

Billhook could hear the sharp patter of Jack as the brothers rowed towards the island. "Of course he'll be back, you dolt. Plenty of skins and oil. Too greedy not to come back."

MIDDLE ISLAND 1825

He wasn't sure about Samuel Bailey. Bailey never looked frightened. Not even when that wave rose right up from the sea like a
fist and punched the whole boat and crew onto the rocks, sucked
back and dropped them again onto the barnacles. Barnacles
good enough to eat but no good coming towards Billhook's face,
straining brine through their teeth. Bailey was the only calm one
that day. He lay in the belly of the whaleboat, facing a mess of
clouds. He was laughing while everyone was white and silent.
And he was laughing when he told Neddy as he found his seat
again that he was going to fucken kill him next time he let the
boat get that close to the rocks on a swell. He knew what had
happened to Neddy's brother on Kangaroo Island and he told
Neddy he'd break his arm over his knee, break it off and chuck it
to the gloamy-eyed devils that hunted seal too.

His laughing and his curses made the crew lighten after their
fright but Billhook could not laugh. There was something in
Bailey's way that shivered him. The next morning it was the
solstice. One of Neddy's black fingers was but a bleeding stump
and he would tell no one what became of it.

THE EYES 1826

The granite cliffs loomed over the whaleboat, streaked black with plant tannins and white with the water of lime. "The Eyes," said Jimmy the Nail, pointing out a deep pair of round holes in the sheer face of stone. "The Eyes."

The Eyes stared down at them as they neared the ledge where a crèche of young fur seals lolled. A single clapmatch, nursing the pups while the other seals hunted, rose to her front flippers as the boat inched closer. Two pups played, flashing their teeth and snaking around each other's sleek bodies. Sal's dog barked at the seals and she shushed him with a quick word. On the lee side of the island, the water close to the ledge was flat. Albatrosses and the big gulls waddled over the surface chasing up a school of whitebait. Muttonbirds sheared the water in quick, black arcs. Jimmy and Smidmore raised their guns and shot the clapmatch and one of the larger pups before the rest of the crèche slipped, yelping, into the sea.

"Better off clubbing those big girls," said Jimmy the Nail as the seal writhed on the rocks, and smirked at the still body of the pup he'd shot. Smidmore rushed to reload, stuffing down wadding and pouring powder from his horn. He sighted again. Billhook and Sal kept their oars sculling at the bow, holding the boat off the rocks. Smidmore's second shot boomed against the island, the bullet sparking on granite and pinging away into the water. He cursed. The seal grunted and squealed beside the dead body of the pup, her chest running with dark blood.

"Take me in," said Jimmy. He clamped his skinning knife between his teeth and looked around for the waddy. Smidmore handed it to him, silent. Jimmy the Nail nodded and climbed over the barrels and stowed mast and sail to the bow, where he stood with his bare feet clutching the gunwales. Billhook and Sal worked the boat in to where water sucked at the rocks. A small surge and the boat bunted the rocks. When the wood hit stone, Jimmy leapt and landed sure on the slippery ledge. Billhook used his oar to push away and the boatload of sealers stood off to watch Jimmy the Nail work.

"Wind's turning," said Smidmore. Out to sea, feathery tips began bothering the water. He looked up at the sky. "Jimmy'll be wantin' to flinch that bitch this week."

After whacking the female seal across the snout, stilling her, Jimmy turned her on one side. He crouched and cut a sure line along the belly. As he cut, the animal's blubber flashed white and then clouded with red. Blood ran over the rocks and into the sea. He peeled back her belly blubber until her guts spilled in silken, colourful heaps over his feet. He continued cutting around the flippers and head until he had a raft of skin and blubber. The seal's peeled body shone red and white. Her eyes rolled back in her head.

"Get that pup aboard," shouted Smidmore to Jimmy. "Wind's coming up." He nodded to Billhook and Sal. "Bring her in."

Sal threw Jimmy a rope and he tied it around the body of the pup. They hauled it in as they would a tuna or shark. Then Jimmy floated the blubber and skin of the clapmatch to the boat. As it rafted closer, Smidmore gaffed at it until it lay draped over the gunwale leaking brine and blood, swilling into the sea that had seeped in since the boat was last bailed.

Jimmy the Nail waited on the edge of the rocks for the boat. By then the wind was blowing her towards the rocks and it took four oars to hold her off. The bow bashed against stone. Jimmy hurled himself into the boat, landing badly against a thwart. Billhook felt the deep bite of his oar as they struggled to get the boat off the rocks. The bow smacked into granite again. The wind grabbed at the stern and started swinging it around towards the ledge.

"Jesus," shouted Smidmore. "Don't let her get around. Fuck, Jimmy. Get an oar."

Jimmy held his head, dazed. Blood ran through the webbing of his fingers.

"Let go of your useless fucking head and get an oar."

Jimmy, shaking blood from his eyes, felt around for an oar. He closed his hand on the waddy, felt its weight and threw it down again. The sea rose under the boat and hefted her sideways onto the rocks. Sal screamed something. Twenty-four foot of men, woman, dog, seal and clinkered wood lay suspended for what felt an age, the oars writhing in the air.

Billhook was on his back and scrambling for his seat when he saw The Eyes again. The boat crunched down as the swell sucked away. They clambered to the windward side of the boat ready for the next wave. Nobody spoke. It was silent but for the wash of water and the second crash of the boat against the rocks. They all knew the next wave would flip the boat and crush them against the rocks. Billhook saw there would be a time when he would dive over to save himself but it wasn't yet. It wasn't yet. The others looked the same. Keep her off. We can get away yet. All of us.

"Alright," said Smidmore. The sealskin slid off the gunwale and into the sea. "When she comes in next, we row like fuck. We row her out, yes? Are you ready?"

FAIRY ISLAND 1826

After a month working the western islands for seal, Boss Davidson left Jimmy the Nail's crew and a whaleboat on Fairy Island, on the far fringes of the Recherche Archipelago. Pigeon, Hamilton, Black Simon, Mary and several others including Kirby as boatsteerer were left on another island to the east. Boss Davidson was taking the schooner on a trade run north to Batavia, a British outpost Billhook had not heard of before, to sell the skins and pick up spice and linen for the Sydney market. After making rough copies of his charts onto canvas for the two boatsteerers, Boss Davidson instructed them to meet him in King George Sound in six months' time.

There was plenty of seal about Fairy Island for a good moon or so. The crew put the boat in on the north shore every morning, rowing the boat around to one of the outcrops and shooting seal while they still had gunpowder. It was good, to shoot seal and not wade around through their barking and snarling and crying, belting them with waddies and watching out for their stinking teeth. Billhook and Bailey swam to the rocks, fast if the blood was running into the sea, looking around them for fins with their knives between their teeth. They hauled the bodies and flensed them until the rocks ran with blood, mixing into streaks of algae and lime from the bush above. Maybe ten seal on a good day. Ten skins and half a barrel of oil. The pups left behind mewled for milk.

Jimmy and Smidmore went into the forest in the centre of the island with axes and returned dragging peppermint branches to fuel the try-pot. They needed plenty of wood to try out the oil, and plenty of salt for the skins. They lit a fire beneath the iron pot and boiled the blubber for hours, skimming off the scum, gaffing out any meat or bones and then ladling the oil into barrels. It would be a long day to try out ten seal but Boss Davidson would be happy.

Billhook set up the drying racks on the beach and watched as the women scraped skins on the long slope of granite above the shoreline. Dancer and Sal sang as they scraped. Although they could have used knives, Sal told him her stone knives were better because they didn't break the hide. The furry ring of hair around Dancer's head bobbed when she nodded at Sal and stopped work to correct Sal's song. She looked to Sal, paused and then sang the same bit again. Sal knew none of her songs and Mary, Dancer's clanswoman, lived on another island now. Dancer repeated the last verse, Sal picked it up, and they began scraping again.

The women wore their wallaby smocks even in the heat of late summer. Salt stained white their feet and calves. On the rocks, scrubbing at the skins, they seemed almost seal-like, lolling about on the rocks. Two seals, slow and brown, crouched over their kin. But he had seen them dancing at night and he had seen them emerge sleek and shining from the water, holding aloft a cray or a New Holland paua. Gleaming and black they were, shining women, alight with the sea or the fire.

He watched Dancer often. Sal would talk to him and tell him things but Dancer refused to speak to the sealers. He didn't even know if she spoke to Jimmy the Nail in the night.

"That Dancer, she knows what she's doing with seal." Jimmy tied off one of the racks and cut the ropey vine with his knife.

His feet squeaked in the fine, white sand. "She's been with the Straitsmen for years now."

"Where is her country?"

"Oyster Bay area? Dunno. Maybe Bruny Island. Johnny got her first. He grabbed her and then later he sold her to that bloke Cooper, after he shot his own woman. Shot her through the stomach, Cooper did, when she was standing in the doorway of his hut one day. Shot her in front of all the other Worthies."

"Why?"

"Make an example of her to the Worthies. This is what happens when you don't work, ladies. That's what Cooper told me. Then he got Dancer and sold her to the Policeman a year or so ago. Cooper's on Kangaroo now. He's got another woman. Onkaparinga woman. I told him he was stupid. Killin' a Worthie. They're worth more alive than they are dead. Some men just don't know how to handle them. When they make trouble fighting, or not working or looking like they gonna mutiny, I just give them a gun. I give them the gun and send them off into the bush. They come back a while later with possums or parrots or pigeons. Happy. Everyone is happy. That's how you handle them. You don't need to shoot them. Dancer's good anyway. Known her for a long time."

Jimmy wrinkled his nose in distaste. "She kills all her babies, is all. Stuffs grass in their mouths the moment they are born. No white man's been able to keep his children with Dancer."

On the first of their days on Fairy Island, they found the cave. Sal's dogs killed and ate the clutch of fairy penguins sleeping in its deepest recesses. Within hours their trident footprints were gone from the white sand as the crew flattened out the floor and built a fireplace at the entrance.

In the evenings they retreated from the constant easterly winds to the limestone cave gaping to the north sky. Their path from the beach to the cave soon wore into a track from their feet and the dragging of barrels. Bushes that Billhook stepped warily around in the first week, remembering the barking barillas from Robbins Island, wore away to sand to give him a clear view for the dreaded snakes. The path widened halfway up the hill and became stony, lined with bright green shrubs sprouting tasty red berries. Here was the cave, made by edges of limestone, the sandy floor falling away down the hill. Here was the cave where they lived, for the moment.

INVESTIGATOR ISLAND 1826

Two moons of working Fairy and the islands clustered nearby brought several barrels of oil, plenty of skins rolled tight and dried with salt, and a sudden silence of live seals. As they had seen no other vessels in the area, Billhook reckoned that his own crew had cleaned them out. Only the bones of their previous kills populated the regular ledges and outcrops they visited.

"West ... Investigator, the Doubtfuls, then King George Sound," said Jimmy the Nail one night. Billhook's shoulders still ached from the day's rowing but the crew were relaxed. They hadn't been skinning or trying out oil for a week or more now and fruitless days were days easy on the body. "We'll pack up tomorrow and ship out the day after."

The next day, after stashing the skins and oil in a remote cave, Billhook stopped to stroke one of the skins, one of the plushest he'd tanned. The ashen tips of the hairs were white against the deep pile of black. Underneath the hair lay the felty soft fur, dense and warming. He held it against his cheek. It bristled slightly before yielding to the warmth beneath. The big female had taken several blows from his whalebone club before she stilled.

Being one of the few who could write, Bailey scratched *Gov. Brisbane* into one of the barrels. "Not that it will stop any bastard," he muttered. He looked up in the dim light of the cave to Billhook silhouetted against the opening, stroking the skin.

"Fuck, you're hard up, you knob. We gotta find you a wife."

"I am keeping this one for my bed," answered Billhook, rolling up the skin.

At dawn Billhook, Bailey, Sal, Neddy, Dancer, Jimmy, Smidmore and the two dogs piled into the boat. They sat on thwarts or piles of nets and canvas. Sal stood at the bow, as she always did when she wasn't on the oars, hanging onto the rope. Billhook had lashed down the heavy iron try-pot in the centre of the boat, beside the masthead, so that it didn't roll about. They tied lengths of canvas to the gunwales, lacing them with rope and tensioning them to make a soft deck, to keep out the sea.

Currents moved at a few knots as the tide swelled around Fairy Island and they let it carry the boat away. There was no wind in the early morning. The men rowed until they were in the open ocean, until the land was only a flat strip overhung with a thin cloud to their north and the island a speck to the east. Dancer huddled her body into the mess of canvas and gear and held tight Sal's big lurcher, moving only to vomit over the side. The piebald terrier dashed about, searching for sea spray to tussle with. In the water, cuttlefish bones dotted with teeth marks bobbed like strange faces in the glittery morning sea, merging into the little colonies of green and yellow weed.

The wind came up midmorning and changed the sea from deep blue to turquoise. Investigator Island was a long sail west from Fairy. They'd lost sight of the mainland by midday and Jimmy the Nail kept checking his compass, saying, "Keep her over, over to port. Thirty miles offshore." Albatrosses and gannets were gathering, attracted by the boat and the lure Billhook dragged in its wake.

As the sun fell, the island lay like a seal on the horizon. Two peaks at either end.

"Is that the island? It's too far north!" Jimmy pulled the canvas map that Boss had given him from his belt and glared at it. He looked up to the island and then to his compass. "Must be it. Not the mainland. That's not the Barrens. That's Investigator Island."

"The Barrens," muttered Bailey. "Jimmy's losing his bearings. That's another day away."

It took three hours after they saw the island to be within its reaches. Reefs spumed and sprayed to their starboard and the sun left only a yellow glow on the horizon. They rounded the nose of the island in the dark, the roar of the swell bashing against the rocks and the flash of white foam their only reckoning. The wind ceased in the island's lee. A quiet little atoll with a black hill to each side embraced them. The sail whispered, whipped and stilled.

Jimmy nosed the whaleboat into the breath whistling over the saddle of the island. He trimmed the sail and tied it off. Smidmore stood at the bow with an anchor.

"Keep her ahead."

Billhook could just see the jagged boulders and the water lapping against them.

"Keep her ahead, another length ... one more length ..."

The rocks were closer, until Billhook could smell the covering of green weed and the earthy funk of the island. The crew, even the dogs, were silent as Jimmy edged the boat towards the rocks.

"Let her off!"

The sail flapped madly and Billhook rushed to furl it, grabbing armfuls of canvas. The anchor splashed. Chain rushed, clanked over the side. As the anchor took, the boat blew off the rocks and held firm against its rope.

In the night, the boat rocked and lulled Billhook's flesh about his bones. He heard waterfall-tinkling against the hull.

"What is that sound? Are we gaining water?" he asked Jimmy the Nail.

Jimmy lurched over the gear to find the bailer. He pulled the coiled rope away from the stern and felt the planks. "No."

"Then, what?"

Jimmy shrugged. "Naiads. Sea lice. Mr Thistle's doomsayer. Go to sleep Billhook."

The bristly sealskin tickled his neck. The anchor chain thudded against its bridle. Jimmy snored, one arm around Dancer's neck, and Neddy whimpered like a dreaming dog.

Billhook slept. Water wraiths played against the hull, thrumming their fingers up and down the planks. Undersea songs trilled in the dark, singing and humming. Little feet clattered on the foredeck. The water wraiths climbed over the sides, small creatures with cat eyes, raking their long fingernails in shining lines of phosphorescence down his neck, over his nubbly nipples and twirled around his stomach.

The quarter moon and naiads slid away when Bailey shook him. "Get up, Billhook."

"Wāhine taipari."

"What? Speak the King's."

"Huh?" Billhook sat up to see a brown gull staring at him from the deck.

"The wind's changed. We gotta put another anchor out."

Billhook sat upright. He could see the spray of onshore waves just to the starboard. Smidmore and Sal looked up from their shared sleeping skin. The boat had swung on its anchor and was blowing onto the rocks. He could feel the anchor loosening its hold on the bottom through every buck of the carvel.

"Get an oar," he shouted. "Let's get her out!"

"Boss said it happens a lot here," Jimmy the Nail murmured, as the boat tugged at two picks east and west. "Anchor up in a sou'-easter at Investigator and the wind goes around to the north in the night." He took a swig from his flask and passed it to Bailey. "Him – he's the only man woke up when she blew around."

Billhook watched Bailey's starlit face wrinkle into a grimace as he swallowed the rum. The weeks on the islands without a razor had produced a beard the colour of kowhai flowers that climbed his cheeks towards his eyes.

Before dawn, Billhook awoke on the pile of skins, nets and canvas and looked around him at the mess of bodies; people and dogs crammed against each other in the clinker boat. The young Pacific gull was still holding place on the deck, clattering its feet on wood. As Billhook wriggled away from the sleeping bodies, the bird eyed him, alarmed, and rose into the air to hover above.

The island glowed golden with the rising sun, its mossy skin bursting with huge boulders. In the sea-blackened saddle between the two hills, surf surged in from the east. Dark shapes moved amongst the rocks on the shoreline. As the day lightened, the seals emerged from their hollows. Two young pups fought, yawning open their mouths to show teeth not yet fetid, yelping and screeching as they gnawed and slapped at each other. Crowning the northern hill, a big male watched over his domain.

Schools of herring drifted around the boat. Billhook found his line in his kit, threaded on some seal meat, threw it over the side. The fish swarmed around his hook and soon he was reefing herring over the gunwales and throwing them into the hollow beside Smidmore and Sal. He'd caught a dozen before a seal swam through the school and the fish peeled away. Sal awoke, slapping the flapping herring from her face. He apologised, but she rose and found a knife and started filleting, using an oar as her board.

Billhook chewed on a piece of raw herring and considered the bull silhouetted at the top of the hill.

"I call 'im down," said Sal. She put her hands around her

mouth and yelped, calling out to the old bull. She laughed uproariously as the seal cocked his head and started lumbering down the hill. "Took 'im all night to get up there, I reckon."

"Keep calling," said Billhook, strapping his waddy over his back. "Keep him coming down."

Sal continued her clapmatch call and the bull lolloped towards them, rolls of fat and muscle. Billhook dived into the water, his scalp tightening with the sudden chill, and swam to the rocks. He slipped and crawled over the glossy black algae, hiding himself behind a boulder on the dark side of the island. He heard the ponderous undulations of the seal as it came towards him, and he clenched the whalebone waddy and his short lance, ready for the kill.

INVESTIGATOR ISLAND 1826

Billhook stood on the peak of the island, looking down to where their boat was anchored. He scratched at his hair. Fine and oily, it was laced silver with lice and salt and felt thick with itchiness. He wondered what the women did to rid themselves of lice. Mud? Oil? There was no lice where he came from until the whalers came. Then it was fat that his mother rubbed through the hair of her children.

About a chain from the rocks, he saw movement, a shining flash of wet skin picked out by the low afternoon sun. But we got them all, all their skins stashed, and still the seal are coming, he thought. No, it was not a seal but Dancer surfacing for air. She shook water from her short, frizzy hair and disappeared again beneath the waves. Sal stood above the barnacles on the rocks, her fur frock flapping in the wind. She was holding a woven bag and watched the waves for Dancer.

The skirts of the island were studded with the peeled carcasses of seals bleeding into the sea. Yellow fat melted away from their flesh in the midday sun, revealing dark mounds of meat and bone covered in squabbling bands of petrels and gulls that rose and fell with the wind. Wherever the wind came from in the days the crew stayed on the island, they could smell the evidence of their slaughter, a rancid rotting of fat and flesh. The try-pot stayed aboard the boat – there was no timber for fire to boil down the carcasses for oil and the nearest landfall was a day's sail away. They kept the sealskins and left the bodies to rot on the rocks.

Dancer rose again from the sea and swam over to Sal, her arms slicing through the waves. Billhook could see her toothy smile as she trod water away from the barnacles, holding aloft a wriggling cray and a fistful of the weed that she ate raw. She threw the cray and the kelp to Sal, who stuffed it into her bag and shouted, waving Dancer back out to sea, laughing.

Billhook knew the area from the weeks he'd spent here. He'd pulled a few paua off those rocks but Dancer was the diver, yes.

This is the reason why the Straitsmen used the Vandiemonian women, he thought. Pallawah women are fearless when hunting the sea bottom.

That Sal, she was no diver and not even much of a swimmer. Sal was an estuary woman whose country was the still waters and fish traps across the channel from Kangaroo Island. Like the men, she preferred something solid: planks, stone or sand beneath her feet. Dancer, whose clumsiness around the fireplace angered the men, she who refused to speak their language and who spent her sea miles vomiting into bilge water, Dancer was a seal in the open sea.

Smidmore climbed up the hill stepping over the tussocks and stones. He stood, as he always did, with Billhook on the side of his good eye and ear. "Movin' on tomorrow, Billhook."

"Yes."

"You seen a big old Noah hanging around?"

For days, small sharks had been slicing around the island, sniffing out the bloodstained rocks and frightening off the herring.

"No. No big ones. Just those whiskeries. A few bronzies."

"I saw 'im this morning ... Christ ..." Smidmore breathed and squinted. "That Dancer down there?"

Dancer dived again and disappeared. Billhook watched Sal shout to Bailey, who was working the boat into shore. Bailey looked startled, out to where Dancer was diving.

"Fuck," said Smidmore. His neck muscles tightened as he watched the water intently. "Fuck. There 'e is. Big bastard."

As each wave rose, the shark appeared in the window of water, its ghostly belly white and the rest of its body shadowy. It did not look to be in a hurry but intent, circling the area where Dancer was diving.

"Where is Dancer?" Billhook called, panic rising in his belly.

"She'll be hiding." Smidmore gave a short laugh.

The shark slid beneath the water, flicking its tail with a splash, almost a salute. Billhook could hear Sal shouting now. Jimmy and Bailey hopped across the rocks towards her and the three stood dark and ragged against the waves. Minutes … hours passed. Smidmore growled deep in his throat when he saw Sal throw up her arms and turn her face away from the sea and onto Jimmy's breast.

"Dancer!" and he started the run down the hill.

Dancer.

Billhook watched Smidmore's black hair flying around his shoulders, his wallaby-clad feet leaping from stone to stone. Smidmore was half the way down when Dancer crawled out of the sea. The waves scraped her over the barnacles. She grabbed at them and hung on as a wave sucked back. She lost consciousness as her face dropped against the stone and razor-sharp shells.

In the evening they lit a fire of dried grasses and fuelled it with penguin skins, bones and dried kelp to keep warm. Sal packed seal fat and ash into Dancer's wounds and spoke to her swiftly in a creole of Vandiemonian and English.

"She was hiding!"

Smidmore nodded to Billhook. "See, Billhook?"

"Dancer hide under the weed. She pull that kelp right over her, like a skin. She lie on her back and watch the shark," Sal waved her arms in circles above her head, "swim all around over top her."

Dancer spoke to Sal in a low voice.

"If she go up, he get her. She don't breathe long time. A bubble and that shark would see her so she not breathe."

Dancer's back and arms were lined with deep gashes, scored by her landfall upon the barnacles. Her body shook with shock and her feet and hands twitched. She said her chest was hurting too. Sal held Dancer's hand and looked at it. "Squeeze," she said. Dancer couldn't move her hand. Sal shook her head. She tore off some canvas and bound Dancer's hand. "She broke her hand. On the rocks."

"No good for nothing else," said Jimmy the Nail, staring at Dancer's bare breasts. "Not 'til she heals." As he did every night when the fire died down, he flicked his finger at Dancer. "Come with me now."

Dancer groaned and rolled her eyes. Silence fell upon the small group as they waited to see if Dancer would defy him. Smidmore and Bailey looked on with interest. Sal and Billhook both shook their heads and then Sal eyed Dancer with resignation. Dancer didn't move.

"Come, I said." Jimmy grabbed at Dancer's bandaged hand and jerked her to her feet. He was still clenching her hand, with Dancer's whining pitched almost to a whistle, as they disappeared into the night.

DOUBTFUL ISLANDS 1826

The black easterly wind strengthened through the day. Sometimes they sailed close enough to land for Billhook to see the stain of grey-blue bushes spreading like clouds across the coast hills. By afternoon the land was misted over with dust and spray and the wind beat at their backs until the boat was hurtling down waves and broaching at the bottom.

As the day wore on and the crew wearied, it became a given that they would not make landfall that night. Though they were close to the Doubtful Islands, the onshore winds meant the breakers would be too big. It was safer to head back out to sea and spend the night away from the rocks. The little boat surfed wave after wave with white foam leering at their peaks when Jimmy the Nail gave the order to go about before the next set came through.

The crew knew what it meant. The sails must be trimmed and they would have to beat into the wind just to hold their position. There would be no sleep. A night of listening for the sounds of the sea changing, listening for the reefs and the bommies, watching for the glint of whitewater in the distance, in a sea that was already a knife-like swathe of cold wind and flying spray and the sound of roaring water in their ears.

As the sun set, the sea turning silver with the horizontal light, Dancer pointed her bandaged hand towards a wave on their port side.

Sal started yelling too. "That big old boy, he's after us!"

The shark surfaced near the boat and turned its head up to them so they could see its glossy black eye, then sank beneath the waves again.

"Put that mutt on as bait," laughed Bailey. Sal hugged the little terrier to her breast and glared at Bailey. "We'd get ourselves a good feed."

Throughout the night, the shark followed them. Sometimes all they saw was the flick of its tail or its snout rising from the water. Once Dancer saw the shark, she stopped vomiting overboard. Instead, she heaved her stomach into the boat and Sal's dogs licked it up.

"Can you take an oar?" Every hour or so, a tired rower would call to be replaced. They would fall back into the belly of the boat and soon be shivering with the cold and pulling skins around themselves, trying to steal a short nap. Another would row then, or handle the mainsail, their oars sometimes missing the choppy sea, skimming through wind and spray. Sal bailed out the boat until she was scraping the tin against the wooden boards.

The men and women were silent except for the occasional, "Can you take an oar?" or "Can you rest me now?" They stared mutely into the darkness, watching for reefs and the shark. Nobody sang, as they often did on their long journeys. They spoke little.

In the middle of the night, the wind changed. Jimmy looked at his compass, squinting, slanting it towards the light coming off the water. "Sou'-west." Billhook could smell the rain before it arrived. A chill roared through the air. He sighed, glad that the rain would flatten out the sea a little but when it started, it blew sideways. It was a stinging rain that soon turned to hail. Small shards of glassy hail hit his face. The crew pulled their caps as far over their eyes as they could and kept rowing. Billhook could no longer feel his fingers.

The hail blew over and out to the north and the rain followed too. Over the flapping of the sail, Billhook heard a knocking sound around the boat. He nudged Jimmy, who started upright from his slumber.

"That bastard," said Jimmy. "He's gettin' cocky."

The shark knocked again.

"I will put out a line," said Billhook.

"Then what'll you do? Bastard'll scuttle us."

"We'll tow him dead."

The rope twanged against the mast an hour later, rattling Billhook from his reverie. He stowed his oar and checked his knots on the line. Thirty yards away, the water bulged and churned with the fighting creature.

"You'd better get on two oars now, Billhook," said Bailey. "Makin' us tow the bastard. Givin' him a free ride, you are."

The rope slackened as the shark swam towards the boat. Then it ripped tight again. For the rest of the night, until the sky whitened with the new day, the rope flicked and loosened and hummed with the might of the great shark. Billhook played, guessing what the shark would do next. His only thoughts were of the shark and the rope and the oars.

The wind dropped just before the dawn. Around Billhook, the crew lay or sat, their faces lined and etched with salt. The oars lay with their handles starred into the centre of the boat. The dogs slept with Sal, the lurcher almost the same length as her body and the piebald terrier lying across her throat. Billhook's hands were crimped into pincers and he could hardly use one to loosen the other. His fingers tingled. He tried to force them straight against the wooden thwart and winced.

Jimmy raised the headsail and they headed for the coast again. Smidmore awoke as the boat's motion changed under sail. "How far off are we?"

Jimmy pointed to the thin strip of land on the horizon. "Morning tea, sir," he said in a toff's voice, then laughed. "Dunno where the Doubtfuls are, though. We could have blown back to Bass Strait in the night."

They sailed along the coast until the sun was above their heads. The Barrens, a long range of black mountains, stayed on their starboard. Finally Billhook sighted the islands hunched against the red cliffs of the mainland. As they drew closer, he could feel the air from the previous night's storm, a cool chill, creeping from the land. It was always warmer out to sea.

The wind had freshened again but they were able to sail around through the channel and into a sheltered cove on the north side of the island. The six of them swung their bodies over the gunwales and into waist deep water, their feet hitting hard white sand, and they pulled the boat into shore.

"This is a good place," said Sal, looking around. "Plenty fish. Trees. Water." She pointed to the green seam of reeds running through the bush down to the beach.

"Let us get this Noah in, hey," said Bailey. "Before all his mates come to the funeral."

As they hauled the fish towards the shore, Billhook saw it was still alive. "We should have tied off its tail and towed it dead," he said. The shark was tired and close to death anyway. It rolled lazily on the beach, twisting the rope around its body, the sand covering its glossy grey skin.

"Must be twelve foot," said Smidmore. "But look how fat! Nearly as round as the bastard is long." He whacked an oar against its nose and the fish slumped, stunned. "That smell ..."

The stench of the dying shark was terrible. When they cut open its belly, the smell became intolerable. Even Jimmy the Nail turned away, his hand over his mouth in a failed effort to staunch his vomit.

With the gaff, Billhook delved into the shark's stomach and reefed out a young seal, bitten in two, a native's broken spear still sticking out of her greasy pelt.

Aramoana 1817

"What fate brought you west?" Smidmore asked Billhook one night.

"The *Sophia*," he answered. "I was looking for the ship," and said no more, for he did not know whose ears were pricked for their mate Captain Kelly.

The sealer William Tucker had washed up on Otakau shores one year before the massacre. Wiremu Heke must have been eleven, a boy, yes, when the Australian whaler Tucker managed to ingratiate himself with Chief Korako and taken a local wife. It was Tucker who one year later led negotiations between the ruddy captain of the *Sophia* and the Chief. Suddenly the Chief suspected Tucker's translation as devious and the deal went awry in the meeting house. Whisperings in the room turned to a rising murmur, then the angry hum of a disturbed hive.

The boy Wiremu remembered Tucker and the day that he was no longer an honorary Otakau. He saw him on the beach screaming, "Captain Kelly! Please! For pity's sake, don't leave me!" as the New South Wales crew and the captain fled to their ship, fighting off the toa, the furious young warriors consigned to battle. Wiremu later saw Tucker hatchetted, and his pieces carried away.

Overnight, the still water shone with the moonlight and the *Sophia* remained at anchor in a dearth of wind to get away, her rigging and ramparts holding men with guns. All night, shots echoed against the sides of the inlet.

At daylight the Australians stormed back through the village armed with guns and crosscut saws. Chief Korako, dead from a bullet through the neck during one of the night's many failed ambushes, was not there to see forty-two of Wiremu's father's boats sawn in half. Even as Kelly's men laboured over the cross saws, covered by guards, their countryman Tucker was being thrown in pieces into an earth oven several hundred metres away.

The crew of the *Sophia* took flaming torches to the end of the village where the warm nor'-easter blew in, and razed the houses. Within an hour scarcely a single dwelling was left standing. Wiremu's father was suddenly smaller, older amidst the screams of the women. He lay on the beach badly injured, his power as master artisan leaching from him, shuddering and bleeding.

Gunpowder won that war, like so many others. Eight days later, fifty warriors washed onto the beaches from the *Sophia* battle. The bodies caught in the brothy corners of the harbour, snagged on trees, bloated in that strange manner of drowned men. Knees bent, legs and arms spread, their bodies plump with water and gases, bullet wounds and cutlass splits marring the faultless etchings on their warrior skins.

No one fished the waters of Aramoana or Whareakeake for a long time. His mother repeated the mantra of tapu waters to Wiremu, weeks later when he was hungry and asked her why they'd not yet harvested the eels.

"He kete kai nga moana katoa."

All the oceans are a food basket.

"Na reira I te wā ke mate tatou, e tika ana kia hoki atu o tatou Tinana ki a Papatuanuku."

We are all born of Rangi and Papa, the Sky Father and the Earth Mother. When we die it is right that our bodies return to Papa.

It was a thin year.

Captain Kelly and his ship were marked. Any ship under his name entering the quiet stretches beyond Aramoana, past the sand spit where the octopus traps lay in shallow waters, did so knowing the grievance, knowing the risk. The Ngāi Otakau knew that Kelly grew fat in New South Wales on the proceeds of his trade, and that he did not feel any pressing need to return.

For the boy, Kelly's blood spilled would have renewed the honour of his broken father but the captain never returned. In late life, his father sat on the marae, watching the young men prepare their waka for this war or that battle. There was anxious talk of the Ngāti Toa coming down from the north after pounamu and power but that was yet to pass. Wiremu's sisters grew into beautiful young women and, with their friends, married or cooked for the tide of sealers and whalers who sailed into their town. Wiremu, the son of a master boatbuilder, he wanted to go to sea and his father knew his hankering.

"You don't say much, do yer?" Samuel Bailey picked at his teeth, threw the twig in the fire and looked curiously at Billhook. Behind Sal, the big dog sighed in its sleep.

Doubtful Islands 1826

Billhook and Samuel Bailey took the boat to the mainland to set fishing nets from the shore. It was early but already the wind had freshened. They rowed towards the rocks, crossing into a windward slop. Bailey stood and steadied himself against the waves. He pointed for the shore and Billhook took his oar. Bailey started flicking directions at Billhook with his fingers, directing Billhook to the place where he wanted to drop the net but Billhook was having none of it. He didn't need navigating. He knew where to go. He worked the boat along a bit until he got to the crevice where water was sucked and spat out again. Closer to where the paperbark trees grew almost to the water. The morning sun turned them a naked-white-man pink. Billhook rowed forward to the north-east, then went astern to the south-east and backed the boat right into the shore. Bailey fiddled with the nets, sorting through the stone anchor and corks.

Their wake arrived after them, swishing into shore. Billhook heard the cawing of the crows and the thump and crack of waves further along the beach. The nets smelt mushroomy as he rowed away, and Bailey played them over the side, the little floats bumping over the gunwales and spilling into the sea.

When he'd thrown over the last float and stone, Bailey looked around and lined up where the island folded into the last saddle of the land, got a bearing on the net's position. Then they rowed the boat back to the shore to wait while the fish meshed.

They found a crescent of stones built facing the sea. Billhook removed a tattered piece of canvas sail that must have been a roof for the shelter, stuffed it into the wall of black basalt, red-lichened rocks and brown granite.

"Whalers," said Bailey, kicking at a glass bottle. "Whalers bloody everywhere."

Billhook sat on the flat stone in the centre of the lookout and thought how in the winter the wind would be at his back and in the spring the water and skies would be clear and bright, not hazy with smoke and dust like it was now in late summer. When the south-westerly would blow at his back, a man could sit here for weeks watching for whales.

Bailey muttered, "Having a look around," and Billhook watched his figure wade through the dense shrubs of fading blue fan-flowers and balls of bright pink against the grey-green bush. Waves curled into the rocks and nudged the boat against the rocks. The breeze blew light spumes of spray and arcs of rainbow across the water. He slapped at a stinging fly, saw the massive sand slips on the hills opposite the bay, rolling fields of stark white dunes. The clouds parted to let the sun in. At his feet lay a midden of paua shell. Ahh.

*

Once he was out of his pants, he tied off the legs to make a bag, crept along wet rocks until he was able to glide out into the sea with a knife between his teeth. It had been weeks since he'd dived for paua, for anything. The cold hit his chest. He struck out for where the lump under the waves made a flat footprint on the surface. Dived down, spilling his hair behind him, found the rock. He could feel the mossy mounds under waving fronds. He knew how to find paua, or muttonfish as the sealers called them. He made his way over the rock, sliding back and forth over the weed with the surge, levering away the shellfish with his blade against stone and felt the sure suck away from the stone. Then he could see the clean oval shape where the fish had been clamped.

Up, gasp, two deep breaths and back down to that rock, thanking the Mother as he levered more paua away from their home and stuffed his trouser legs full of clicking, oozing meat with the smell of a woman on them. He climbed out of the water, dragging his catch along behind him, blinking the salt from his eyes to see Bailey stumbling down the hill towards him.

Bailey's face looked strange, set and hard. He was scanning for the quickest way to the boat. He was carrying something; an animal. It wriggled under his arm.

"Get the boat. Get it."

Then the naked, struggling child kicked at him and he almost dropped her.

Billhook did as Samuel Bailey told him. He swam to the boat and rowed it to the rocks, backed it in so that Bailey could climb in, dragging the child after him. The girl was whining and grunting with fear and Bailey put his face close to hers until her running nose nearly touched his. He just growled at her. Nothing else. He growled at her like a dog and she was silent.

"Better get that net up, Billhook." Bailey looked behind him to the shore. Smoke rose in a thin, vertical line from behind the hill, blowing off with the sea winds.

Billhook hauled up the net, silver sickles of herring and yellow-eyed mullet flashing and writhing in their cotton bonds, into the deck of the boat, pulling the boat away from the rocks.

Lean black men ran down to the shore, shouting. They began throwing spears into the water but their reach would not answer. The boat was too far away and the spears slid into the water.

"A kid, Bailey. Why a kid?" Billhook's voice sounded vague

and thin. He struggled to give it more strength when he spoke again. "What do you need a kid for?"

"Prefer a woman myself," said Bailey. "But she didn't wanna come."

Bailey's trousers were bloodied and wet. There were flecks of flesh on his bare feet. Billhook looked at the little girl. She didn't seem to be injured. From under Bailey's arm she stared at Billhook's nakedness with flared eyes. She stared at the inky spirals that the tattooist had carved into his buttocks before he left for New Holland. Her fleshy, hairless cleave and her staring eyes made his tattoos, his very flesh, dirtied and, quite strangely, dishonourable.

Billhook knew when he saw the blood on Bailey's trouser cuffs that he should never have obeyed him. That he should have gone back to the Doubtfuls and left Bailey to the blackfellas and their spears. But too late.

"You done well, Billhook," said Bailey, as Billhook dumped the anchor and the last of the net into the boat and collected his oars, the spears well out of range now. "I owe you."

Billhook rowed against the wind once they moved out of the sheltered bay. Bailey sat in front of him, holding the girl. She stared at Billhook, terrified. He tried to say something gentle but his words came out as a grunt and he gave up, taking a bead on the smoke rising from behind the hill to keep his course straight. They moved closer to the island.

Jimmy the Nail met them in the shore of the cove. Billhook threw him the rope. Jimmy whistled low when he saw the child.

"Whatcher got there, Bailey? Dinner? What the hell did yer think yer doing?"

Bailey repeated something of what he'd said to Billhook and picked up the girl, trying to climb over the side and hang on to her at the same time. She shrank away from Jimmy standing in the water, her arms flailing, her legs pushing against the planks.

"Get one of the Worthies," said Bailey.

Sal was already coming down the hill, then Dancer followed her, her wild halo of hair bobbing as she walked. They stared at Billhook's tattooed nakedness and then they saw the girl. Dancer stood in the water and became quite still. Sal's face crumpled. She shook her head and wailed, "No, no, no," and broke into her own language.

Jimmy the Nail cuffed her. "Talk her out Sal, or she'll go over the side." To Bailey, he said, "Though she'd be better off in the drink than with you, you fucking kiddy crimper."

The women hauled the girl into the water. Dancer picked her up and piggybacked her to the shore. They stepped out of the water and walked along the beach until they reached the damp corner where the spring came out of the hill.

Billhook stayed in the boat. He sorted through the net, unmeshing the fish that were dumped into the boat in their haste. He pushed their heads through their tight bonds, their air sacs bursting from the pressure. Scales fell away from the mullet as he pushed them through. He sharpened his knife and set to cleaning the fish, throwing the guts overboard. Petrels and gulls clamoured and fought over the scraps in the water. He dropped the cleaned fish into the bailer full of salt water. A skin of oil clouded on top. He sharpened his knife again. He would not think about the girl. But he kept looking over to where she sat with the women near the spring.

*

The two women and the girl sat in the sand. Dancer reached into her bag and showed the girl a ball of ground seed paste. The child looked at the ball with its flakes of husk and seeds. Her eyes travelled from Dancer's bandaged hand, up her plump arm with its scrapes and gashes, to Dancer's barnacle-slashed face. Her breath sucked in and then came out in great racking sobs, snot and tears gathering on her chin.

Sal hauled over the big dog to sit beside the girl and held out the girl's hand to stroke her.

"What is your name?"

The girl shook her head. The dog rolled over and Sal picked fleas off the clear skin around his genitals.

"Sal not nice to him," Dancer said to the girl. "Sal tiall wee pella kaeeta. She beat him and throw him into the sea."

Sal frowned at Dancer.

"What is your name?" she asked again.

Silence.

DOUBTFUL ISLANDS 1826

"Another titter?" Jimmy the Nail picked at his scabby knuckles and then squinted at Billhook. "You want me to get another woman for that kid thief?"

"Tell him he can have the next one. A bleeder."

"Didn't you help him snatch her?"

Billhook closed his eyes. "She is little. Too little for Bailey. Let the Worthies look after her. She can work."

"Bleeders are one fuck away from being with child, Billhook. That's why Bailey got her little, like that."

"She's too little. He will hurt her."

Jimmy laughed. "... *hurt her* ..." He laughed again and then coughed. He swept one arm around the bay across from the island, to the dark mountains beyond, the unravelling threads from his canvas sleeves whispering against his wrist. "Tell me Billhook. Do you see law here? Do you see some knob with a wig, a hanging judge, a captain with a gun, a preacher, a peeler, a keeper of my fucking conscience?"

"No," said Billhook.

"Well, what then?"

"No one here but us, Jimmy."

"Well, tell me. What do you want me to do then?"

"Tell him. Tell him he can't have her. Tell him he can have the next one we get."

"What the fuck does this have to do with me?"

"You are boss," Billhook nodded at him. "Trouble with the

Worthies, if he takes her."

"Trouble if he don't," Jimmy sighed. "And we all done things. Bailey's not the first tar with a black child wife."

"It's different to shooting some blacks at their fires and getting out."

Jimmy narrowed his eyes at Billhook.

Billhook knew about Jimmy killing those black men on the cape near Kangaroo Island. As well as Pigeon, Sal had told him of a gang of men going to the mainland, hunting for women. One woman with an infant at her breast was stolen away to Kangaroo Island and passed around the camp that night. After they raped her, she crawled away from the sleeping men, gathered her baby from Sal and was never seen again.

"She swam," Sal had told Billhook. "She swam with baby on her back, long, long way home. Baby died." When Sal said that, she fingered the little white skull at her throat.

"This is different," Billhook said to Jimmy. "Bailey getting a kid like that. I'm not like Bailey. I don't need a poor kid. You are not like Bailey but you have Dancer. There will be trouble. Trouble with the women." Billhook fought away the desperation from his voice.

"He should just take her back then," Jimmy said. "Or drown her. Either way, we'll have to ship out of here if we can't go ashore. Just be thankful those blackfellas don't have a boat or we'd be stuck like pigs in our sleep."

Bailey left the child alone. Wherever she was, Splinter the lurcher, the piebald terrier or one of the women were beside her. Billhook wondered if Jimmy had talked to Smidmore because neither men made use of Sal or Dancer at the same time. Bailey seemed to retreat from his claim on the girl but Billhook saw him watch her, and snake his eyes at Sal, especially Sal. He looked to have it in for her and whenever he had a chance, he would aim a kick at one of her dogs.

Doubtful Islands 1826

For the next few moons they roamed the islands and rocky headlands looking for seal and watching out for the natives' fires. The days became shorter, the air stilled and cleared as regular rains cleaned away the dust. They worked to the east and west of the islands. Jimmy watched the coast through his looking glass for seal on the rocks. When he shouted, the men slowed at their oars or slackened the sails and they cruised in to where the sea swayed against the land. On days when the water sparkled with sunlight, they could see the seals stark against the rocks, rolling about like maggots. But on days when the westerlies blew over the land and harried the waves offshore in fizzy rainbow plumes and blew the rain sideways, the seals were not so easy to sight.

Neddy and Smidmore came back from exploring with news of a cave on the seaward side of the second island. "Full of seals, a dozen at least," said Smidmore. "They're resting up in there. Ready to get cornered."

"Let's go then," said Jimmy the Nail. "Before the tide comes in."

They packed wick, a crock of seal oil and extra ropes into the boat. They crammed cooked seal meat and damper into their pockets. Sal directed Dancer to stay behind with her big hound and the child.

"What are you bringing the runt for then?" Bailey asked, nodding at the terrier.

"Keep you company," Sal grinned but her eyes were dead.

"You like the little ones, yes?"

Smidmore snorted with laughter and Bailey's jaw tightened.

The cave gaped its enormous maw at sea level but the tide was low. Neddy pointed out the bridge where two men could stand, while the others went into the cave. They would have to swim into there, to get the seals.

Bailey and Jimmy jumped overboard feet first and rose to the surface, their hair slicked over their faces, spouting water from their mouths. They swam to the bridge, each holding a rope that spooled from the deck of the boat. Billhook and Smidmore placed match tins and the oil-soaked wicks under their beanies, strapped clubs over their backs, and eased themselves into the water. They swam past where the two other men were climbing onto the low rocks at waterline in dripping shirts, their clubs readied, and continued into the cave. Billhook swam on his side, reaching his right arm towards the darkness, keeping his head dry. He couldn't see further than a body's length in front of him. He willed himself not to turn and look for the light. He knew it would destroy any dark vision he had. Water sucked at the rocks as the light swell moved into the darkness. He could smell the seals but he couldn't see anything, only feel the rocks beneath his hands and feet. It became shallow. He heard the shuffling of bodies against stone and Smidmore climbing, dripping, across the submerged rocks behind him.

A breathing, a snorting, as the seals scented the men.

Billhook stood up on a slippery rock and felt above him for some dry stone. He struck a light, put it to the wick, and orange light flared against the walls.

"Look," Billhook whispered to Smidmore, pointing to the ceiling.

The ceiling bulged with boulders held together with mud or clay and the light wavered against the concentric circles cut into the stone, perfect round holes pocked into the granite in symmetrical lines. Light glittered against hovering droplets of water about to fall.

"What are they? Someone was here once. Who would live in this wet hole?"

"Before the seas rose up maybe," said Smidmore. "Before the Great Flood. Let's get on with it."

Around them seals, males and females and pups, lay across the rocks at shoulder height, on the lower, wetter rocks, and rolled in the small pools at the men's feet. A small seal child, its eyes glowing orange against the flaming wick, teeth and saliva flashing, turned to Billhook and shrieked in alarm.

The two men worked as fast as they could, before the wicks burnt through or the seals escaped. They crashed their clubs across whiskered snouts and cleaved open heads. The older seals shouted and barked and the pups gave low-pitched screams as the men stepped and slipped between the rocks. The stench of the seals' breath, their blood and their fear, mingled with the earthy, weedy scent of the cave. Billhook heard Bailey's shouts and then Jimmy's laugh as the first escaping seals were slaughtered at the cave's mouth.

After a while Billhook felt water rising up his trousers, so that wherever he went, his knees were wet. Around him dead seals floated, knocking against his legs and swilling against the walls. The light flared once and then they were in darkness.

"Bring in the rope," said Smidmore and Billhook stumbled along the dark passage, towards the mouth of the cave and the blue sky. He saw the silhouettes of Bailey and Jimmy hanging onto the stone bridge. Outside, the boat bobbed on the rising swell as Sal and Neddy hauled a brace of bound seal pups aboard.

Swell burst into the cave. Jimmy and Bailey jumped onto

higher rocks at the mouth as a wave threatened to suck them both out to sea.

"Rope," shouted Billhook and Jimmy climbed down after the next wave to retrieve the coil of rope. He hung on to one end and Billhook turned back to the dark tunnel and the stench of dead seal. Hanks of wet, tarred rope played out from across his shoulders. He could hear Smidmore dragging a carcass towards him over the rocks, water dripping and the odd, anguished cry of an injured animal.

They hauled nine seals bigger than men as close as they could to the mouth of the cave, tied them off and shouted to Jimmy and Bailey to pull them out. Smidmore cursed as he stumbled about. Billhook repeatedly bashed his shins against the slippery rocks and then crushed his big toe in a crevice. His eyes never adjusted with the constant movement from light to dark. He began thinking the two gatekeepers had it good until he saw Bailey get knocked over by a wave, hit his head and lose his rope. It was bloody work all round.

Once the stress of hauling out the seals to the boat was over, the men grabbed the rope and were hauled themselves. Bailey missed his rope, cursing. He had to swim. Sal and Neddy had let the boat blow off the shore. Billhook, already aboard, watched Sal's curious satisfaction. She would have been happy to see a huge fish rise out of the water and swallow Bailey whole.

"Go in and get him, come on," said Jimmy.

"Ahh, he's alright," said Smidmore.

The boat continued blowing away from Bailey, swimming over the chop, his shirt billowing behind him in the water, trying to catch the end of the rope that lay on the surface like a taunt, a little wake behind it. Finally Billhook and Jimmy took the oars and rowed in to get him. Bailey gripped the gunwales. The terrier, having been kicked so many times by the man, took his chance and leapt forward to bite his hand. Bailey hauled himself over the side. When he wriggled into an upright position, he was furious.

The little dog growled at Bailey. Hardly a raised lip but enough. Bailey looked over to Sal, grabbed an oar and it fell behind the strength of his rowing arm across the nose of the piebald terrier, a killer blow for the old dog who fell to the bowels of the boat, silent, his gnarled paws twitching.

Sal shrieked and went for Bailey. She grabbed his wet shirt and bloodied his nose, whilst he was one-armed trying to stow the oar. His fleshy thud into her face flew in amongst all this. A creamy slop rocked the boat, broaching it sideways. Seal carcasses rolled to one side. Billhook fell to starboard against Smidmore, who swore at him, trying to bring the boat about and head back into the chop.

The little whaleboat fairly throbbed with grunting, shouting men, Sal with her bloodied face and the dead piebald dog.

"I'll get that lurcher next and you'll have no dog to look out for her then," Bailey said to Sal.

DOUBTFUL ISLANDS 1826

In the night Billhook heard shouts and the clanking of an anchor chain. The dawn revealed a whaling barque holed up in the lee of the island, sitting in the calm waters like a mirage.

He kindled a fire and lit it, holding his hands over the flame, waiting for the sun to come over the island and warm him. Winter was setting in and the ground was chill beneath his bare feet. He looked back out to the whaler. Three of its spars were broken and one of the furled sails looked torn.

"Yanks." Jimmy appeared beside Billhook and he too reached for the fire. "They'll have some rum."

Billhook didn't ask what the trade would be. Skins he hoped, but already he knew.

"We visit them, before they visit us," said Jimmy.

The whalers looked tired as they lined the deck and waited for the small boat of sealers to come alongside. They smelled bad too. The whole ship reeked; even the stays were coated in whale oil.

"The boat ahoy!" shouted the second mate.

"Permission to board!" shouted Jimmy the Nail, and a black jack threw down the rope ladder. Sal, Dancer, Neddy and the little girl stayed in the boat, while the men climbed aboard the whaler.

Billhook tried to hide the assault on his nostrils but still, the whalers smirked at his attempt.

As he trod the boards, he realised that in all the filth and stink, the deck was scrubbed clean.

Jimmy the Nail shook the captain's hand. "James Everett."

"Jeremiah Gleeson, of the *Sally*. Who are you working for in these parts?"

"*Governor Brisbane*. We're meeting Boss Davidson at King George Sound in one month." For a Kangaroo Islander, Jimmy the Nail sounded strangely formal addressing the American. Billhook realised that he had slipped back to his whaling way of speaking with the master.

Gleeson laughed. When the other men heard the name of the sealers' mother ship, they laughed too, their faces cracking around their beards, stumps of teeth and yellow tongues. The only man who didn't laugh was a mad man who paced, muttering into his scorched hands.

Jimmy looked to Bailey, at Billhook and then back to the captain, puzzled and angry. "Is there a lark here?"

Some of the men were still sniffing but they settled at the look on Jimmy's face. The captain disappeared into the hold and returned with a newspaper. "*Hobart Town Gazette*. We were there three weeks ago. Shipping news."

He opened to page three and poked at a column. "'The *Governor Brisbane* has been seen on the north-west coast of New Holland with only two men and the master on board," he read aloud. "But then, further down, it writes, 'The *Governor Brisbane* has arrived at Batavia' ... ahh ... 'Some suspicions were entertained at Batavia that the *Governor Brisbane* ... In consequence of this, and some circumstances of a doubtful nature, which appeared on examination of her papers, she was seized, and put under the charge of a guard ship lying in the roads.'"

"What does all this guff mean?"

"My friend," the captain addressed Jimmy the Nail with genial broad vowels, "it means your boss has shafted you. He's accused of piracy, of trying to sell the *Governor Brisbane* in Batavia. He won't be back for you anytime soon, was never planning to."

Billhook remembered the Blunt twins at the bay near the islands, the upside down tattoo on Jack's arm, and Tommy's pleas for Boss Davidson to return. The meagre pile of skins that Boss took to Batavia.

"That fucking dog," said Smidmore.

"But he'll want the skins and oil," said Jimmy, his jaw working as their predicament became clear. "If they let him go, he'll come back for the skins. There's money in them."

"The market bellied out a few months back, mate, when the Brits took the tariff off foreign skins. He won't be wanting skins. He probably knew that."

Silence then, as the gang realised that as well as being abandoned, they weren't to be paid their lay.

"Want some work?" asked the captain.

Billhook, Smidmore and Jimmy took in the oil-stained stays, the stinking ship, the sores about the mouths of the men and the dull looks to their eyes.

"What happened to him?" Jimmy pointed to the man muttering at his hands. "He don't look so good."

"He's mad. Got swallowed by a whale and he's not been right since."

While the captain launched into the story of the man who was swallowed by a whale, Billhook looked around at the crew. A tattooed man was watching him intently. North Islander, judging by the moko and the shape of his face, his squat, strong legs and curly hair knotted on top of his head. Billhook nodded to him and he nodded back. Good to get some news later, he thought.

Gleeson and Jimmy began negotiating the rum, tobacco and women. The captain peered over the side at Sal, Dancer, Neddy and the child. "You can leave the kids out of the deal," he said, frowning with distaste. "Get some trousers on her too."

He went down into the hold again and returned with a small pair of canvas slops. "She can have these."

"A kid's trousers?" Jimmy the Nail looked around at the crew. "Don't see any naked cabin boys aboard, Captain."

Every man standing on deck bowed their heads. The mad man set up a howl. "The lad went over the side, the day Bartley got swallowed by the whale," said the captain. "A sea burial off the coast of Otakau."

"You took the clothes off his dead body?"

"He didn't need them where he was going," the captain shrugged. He nodded towards the child. "And this one does."

"They won't take long to blow," Smidmore said to a furious Sal, as they rowed back to the island. "Dinna worry girl. They've not had a woman in an age."

Jimmy the Nail whooped. "We gotta spree, lads! An evening of drink and song to ease our sorry situation." He tweaked Dancer's ear as she helped the child into her new trousers. "Make the most of it won't you, Dancer. No crying now."

"So long as those dirty bastards don't turn 'em into fireships. Don't want no pox on my house," said Smidmore and Jimmy laughed.

Billhook wasn't listening to Smidmore and Jimmy's banter as he pulled at the oars. Otakau. Hearing the name of his home country spoken aloud sent a shock through his body. Gleeson had come from Otakau.

*

"We'll be wintering about these parts," said Gleeson that evening, settling himself into a comfortable position by the fire. "Going after the humpbacks until October, then offshore after that, off the shelf after some fin, then home to New Bedford." He seemed relaxed and pleased with himself. "It's been a good season."

The first mate, a burly white man with woolly hair, gave a small cheer. "That'll make it eighteen months," he said.

Smidmore tuned his fiddle and the second mate took a harmonica from his pocket and grinned at him. Despite the disappointing treatment of them by Boss and the ripening scent of the whalers warming by the fire, the sealers were exhilarated by the strangers after so long in their own company. Sal and Dancer had snared some potoroos and the Americans brought tobacco, rum and fresh vegetables from their itinerant gardens along the coast.

"Wiremu Heke," Billhook said to the North Islander. He grasped his hand.

"John te Marama." The two men touched their noses together, staring into each other's eyes. Then they squatted on their haunches and began to converse in language.

"Where is your home?"

"Kiri Kiri ... but now the missionaries have moved in, we have to go away to make any trouble or fun! The women and the old men, they like the singing in the church. Me, not so much and that Parson ... they call him the Flogging Parson."

"Ahh! I've heard of him! My country is Otakau."

Marama nodded. "I thought so. I saw you when Gleeson said it. And now I know your name ..."

"Did you go there, after ..."

John te Marama nodded again. "After we cut Bartley out of the whale, his skin was burnt by the whale's stomach juices. His fingerprints are gone now but when he came out he looked like he'd been skinned all over. His body was all red. We took him to the village and the women healed his skin with special leaves and smoke. They couldn't fix his soul though. Fled from his body."

"Who did you see there? Did you see my father? The old boat-builder. Did you see a woman called Nga Rua?"

Marama paused. "The woman who healed Bartley was Nga Rua. She's a good woman, Wiremu." Marama smiled. "Still cheeky she is. But Wiremu – while we were there, your father died. He died suddenly, in his sleep. Your mother said it was the white man's fault. That he died in her arms, broken. Nga Rua will never forgive those men who destroyed her husband. She said this thing at the tangihanga. I am sorry, Wiremu."

Billhook dropped his head into his chest and ran his hands along his scalp. Oh my father ... gone.

"There is more news," Marama said gently. "We went back to the North after we left Otakau. The Ngāti Toa, Te Rauparaha's men. They are coming."

"Te Rauparaha?" Billhook snapped up his head. All he had ever heard of that man was the carnage he left behind, the heads on sticks, children impaled on pikes and left facing out to sea to warn off his foes. Te Rauparaha and his toa were the bogeymen, the angry ghouls that he had only ever heard hushed talk about. Bloodstained teeth and handfuls of women's hair. "He's coming?"

"He wants control of the South Island – and your pounamu. He's preparing to invade. I know this because he saw the Parson in Port Jackson when he went there to get guns. When he gets to Otakau he will walk the country claiming ownership. Anyone who resists will be slaughtered. His toa are too many."

"My people have guns now, from the whalers. Maybe ..."

"There are too many," Marama said with simple fatalism and felt around in his kit bag. "I am very happy to find you, Wiremu."

"I'm not so happy with your news, brother." Billhook took a deep draught of rum and felt it burn down his gullet.

"It is terrible to have to say these things. Nga Rua thinks that you are working out of Hobart Town."

When Marama said familiar names like "Hobart Town" or "Otakau" out loud, it warmed Billhook. It was an age since he had talked with his own people.

"When she heard that the *Sally* was going to Van Diemen's Land, she honoured me and invited me to your father's tangihanga. Later she asked me to find you and give you this. So you see, if I had not found you, then Nga Rua would be unhappy with me and she is the last woman I would want to offend."

Oh Sally, she'n the gal that I love dearly, the men sang.
Way oh, sing Sally oh
Sally she'n the gal that I love dearly,
Hilo Johnny Brown stand to your ground.

Just out of the firelight it was quite dark but Billhook knew what John te Marama placed in his palm without looking. The weight, the cool, glossy curves and stiff strands of ancient sinew against his fingertips told him that it was the orca tooth necklace.

Oh Sally, she'n my bright mulatta
Way oh, sing Sally oh
Sally gal she do what she ought to do
Hilo Johnny Brown stand to your ground.

DOUBTFUL ISLANDS 1826

Billhook climbed to the highest part of the island, away from the fires, past the sweet-scented flannel flowers and over sheets of cool granite. There was no moon, yet. He climbed until he could see the dark mountains crowding the long white bays in the east. He lit a small fire and sang his father's waiata.

Sal's lurcher followed him and slumped into the grasses eventually, twitching with hunting dreams while Billhook sang and sang, fed by grief and rum. Finally he quietened and the words, laughter and music travelled up the hill to him.

"What's he doing?"

"Blackfella stuff."

"Leave him alone."

"Heathen."

"You're no man to talk ... fucking heathen yerself."

"Who's got that Sal?"

"Got a dud deal with that cut-up woman."

"Cries all the time, she do."

"And then we fastened on the bull."

"Try some o' this."

"And after a day we dragged him alongside and flensed him."

"You never want to see a face like his in yer life, mark my words."

"That bull's stomach was wrigglin'."

"The lad Kim."

"I don't want no fireship whore."

"He came up out of the sea like an angel, Kim did."

"Like an angel, he was."

"This one here, she looks like an angel."

"Where'd you get the kid from? She's real pretty."

When Billhook heard that he galloped down the hill, stumbling over mounds of grasses and rocks, cursing as best as he'd learnt from the sealers. He'd forgotten all about her. He stopped again to listen.

Bailey.

"Well, don't I get a go at Sal, then?"

"Nah. You got a fucking useless prick, Bailey, and where's your rum?"

"I'll earn me some."

Splinter woofed at Billhook's side.

And so Billhook ran again, until he was standing on the outside of the firelit party, panting and bloodied, breathing in the alcohol fuming from the men's bodies. He saw the captain unconscious, the little girl gathered onto the first mate's lap, him undoing the flap of his pants and Bailey looking on, smiling like he had in his mind the sweet memory of something good. Billhook had never seen Bailey smile before. He'd seen the look on that child's face though, that look the day she was stolen. Beyond the light of the fire and Smidmore's fiddling, he could hear the grunts and crying of Sal and Dancer and the men.

He reefed the child from the whaler by one arm, yanking her up to his chest until he could feel her heart beating against his. She screamed with pain and started up a whine. He did not know the deep, steady authority in his voice when he said, "No one! No one touches this child."

The music stopped. John te Marama, for no other reason than he was Billhook's countryman, leapt to his feet and glared lizardly around at the group, daring anyone to act. No man spoke. They were all too shocked or drunk or both, though Jimmy the Nail and the captain were disturbed enough in their sodden slumber to roll over and snore deep draughts.

Billhook withdrew from the light with the child still clamped to his chest, as Smidmore struck up a new tune on his fiddle.

So the ne'er do well,
The son o' a swell,
He's bin cuckolded
By a sharpish blackfella.

Laughter.

Billhook stood in the dark beyond the bed of skins in the tea-tree forest where two men laboured over Dancer and Sal. He listened to the whalers climax with their odd, boyish whimpers, and watched their shadowy figures shamble away towards the fire still doing up their trousers. He shushed to the whimpering child. Then he gave the women a low whistle. They came out of the forest towards him, both of them limping, stooped and beaten.

"Get your skins," he whispered in English. The child whined softly. "We'll go the other side of the island tonight."

Doubtful Islands 1826

"You pulled out her arm," Sal said to Billhook.

Despite the darkness he saw the accusing flash in Sal's eyes. "Ae?"

"You pulled out her arm. Now do as I say, Wiremu! Just do as I say and quick!"

Sal gestured for him to distract the child, anything, anything, away from her port side. While the girl sat on a smooth chunk of basalt weeping with pain and cradling her left arm, Billhook obeyed Sal and took the only prop he had, the orca necklace. He rattled it against his palms, shaking the teeth against each other. The child turned and looked at Billhook, trying to see where the sound came from. He reached the white teeth towards her and as her hand stretched out, Sal, in one quick, brutal movement, grabbed the child's other arm, twisted it and pushed it back into its socket.

The child screamed. Then her cries fell away to whimpers of relief.

Dancer nodded and said something in her language.

"No one to look after her tonight, Billhook. Dancer, she said that," said Sal.

"Will she be, will her arm be ... where I pulled her ...?"

"She will be sore." And in the first moment of collusion with Billhook since the day that she greeted him at Kangaroo Island, she grinned and said, "But plenty, plenty sore if you didn't pull out her arm."

They waded through prickly waist-high scrub and fell down muttonbird burrows until they found a place far enough away from the party of men; a reedy hollow where the only sounds that reached them were the wind and the swell against the granite. Even the penguins were quiet. In the morning, before dawn, Billhook left the women, the child and the dog and trekked over the penguin tracks back to the camp.

The scuffed dirt around the fire was littered with sleeping bodies, their faces cracked and the bush flies beginning to find them. It looked as though they'd been fighting, with blue bruises gathering on reddened brows and chins. Black flies clustered around the tattered remains of the first mate's ear.

Bailey was the only man awake, lying on a skin, still drinking from a bottle of rum, so far gone that he had come back again.

"Thanks for stealing me the child, Billhook," he slurred. "She'll make me some money one day, not this day, but one day. Beautiful girl. She reminds me of Elizabeth."

A kennel confession it was, because talking to Billhook did not count for Samuel Bailey. Billhook heard Bailey's accent change, from rough tar language, to the talk of some white men Billhook had met; the Englishmen with no beards, and scribblers in their soft hands. It made him listen; Bailey's slipping into another world. Billhook stepped over the captain to kindle the fire with brushwood. He blew on the coals and watched the curl of smoke seep through the twigs. He knew Bailey wanted to talk and he felt disgusted already with his wanting to hear it.

"It's against the law to sell a person these days." Bailey struggled into a sitting position and nodded over to the tea-tree forest where he must have thought the women were sleeping, worn out from their labour. "Not illegal to own a slave, only illegal to sell one." He slugged from the bottle of profit. He breathed in and started.

"That Weed. Weed because she wee'd all down my leg when I got her. She's a fey sprite. Never seen a girl so pretty except one ... she reminds me of those children, like beggars they were but worse, trying out the streets, just babies. Where were their mothers? Couldn't see what was going on under their own noses, too drunk, too poor, fathers away fighting Frenchmen. T'was not my fault Billhook. They needed a feed and a bed. Mine own mother so ill with the melancholia and a doctor who gave her pills. Father worked at the victualling office, supplying the war. He watched those children come and go, he did. He knew which ones needed his help. He would have them home – but only for short stays lest they stole something. Got so the kids would come up to me in the street and ask for food and a bed. I'd run home and ask my father. 'Is it William?' He would ask. 'Solomon? No, not that Solomon boy. He's trouble. Elizabeth. Go and get me Elizabeth.'

"So I'd find her. That girl, eight or nine, she would follow me home in the cold, with rags wrapped about her feet. Father would take her hand and lead her down the hallway. The day the war ended I was sickly, had messed my own bedclothes and the servants were sleeping. Mother was sleeping. She always slept. I walked down the hallway towards a crack of light, dragging my stinking vomity blankets.

"Elizabeth looked straight at me when I opened the door. She still looked hungry ... no not hungry. Nothing. Elizabeth was on my father's lap, he with a blanket over them both and the fire blazing merrily. He was lurching and squirming ... she didn't look hungry, she looked pinched, like someone had pinched her face into a point, pinched her so hard all the blood had gone out of her.

"Now that was no hanging offence, Billhook. No money changing hands there. Those kids just needed a feed. Ha! They got one too. I was a boy of twelve when old Scarface quit his war and I wanted to go to sea with the merchants but father wanted me to complete an education. He must have wanted me to get him kids, too. Still I took to skiving off school and going down to the docks. Watching the ships coming back from the Antipodes and the Americas. Watch those tars disembark and head off for the drinking houses or the brothels or their homes where the wives were. But I was still tied to my home by father's wishes and the money that went with it.

"I saw Elizabeth one day, at the docks. She must have been about eleven or twelve by then. She looked at me askance and I knew she knew who I was but she didn't want to say. Her eyes were gone all hard and grey. They were once so pretty and blue. Her lips were so full and now they pressed tight. The pox was about her mouth and she seemed a bit wobbly on her feet, but not in the manner of a drunkard, though she took a bottle from her skirts and tipped it above her head, poured red wine into her mouth so her lips bloomed again. No she didn't walk like a drunkard. She walked through the piers on air, not quite touching the ground, not wafting in an unearthly way but like the girl didn't want congress with such coarse things as cobbles and planks.

"She walked through crowds of men. Her skirt was fine red velvet but the hem was ragged and torn. A gift from a john, no doubt. She wore a green waistcoat and a shirt that was white once."

Bailey stopped, returning to that day in his mind.

"Her hair was orange and her skin pale. She walked by a mob of tars and they all stopped talking. They turned to look after her. One nudged the other and then he caught up with her. She didn't need to hustle, with those nice baby tits. The man caught her arm and she turned to him with a smile trained to turn upon any strange sailor she needed money from. For the next bottle, I suppose. Something to eat. Tobacco. Some rouge for all that unwrecked beauty. I watched her walk away with the sailor towards the bridge under croft, hips swaying, slim hips swaying like a child trying to be a woman, by the sailor's side."

Bailey slugged from the bottle of rum, spluttered and then farted. "So I was right. She was just a whore." He nodded again towards the tea-tree forest. "Just like those whores. Little Lizzie was always a whore, giving up herself to any scrawny syphilitic tar. She was better off being fed by father had he not lost interest in her when her tits sprouted. But ... looking back ... that day the *Elk* came in fresh from the Cape and looking for crew and that's how I came to be in the colony. Without father's blessing. Although he victualled an entire navy, he failed to victual me for my troubles."

He turned to stare at Billhook with scorched blue eyes. "He said something odd the day after I saw him from the hallway. He said, 'Samuel, what you observed is an ancient manorial right.' *An ancient manorial right.* But I'll never live in a house again, Billhook, let alone a manor. The halls ... the hallways do me in."

Doubtful Islands 1826

Jimmy, Smidmore and the captain spent an age in earnest debate, on the beach beside the whaleboat. The captain, with his florid face and waistcoat over his corpulent, barrel body looked as though he was winning. Jimmy's rags and kangaroo skins, his scarred face and Smidmore's long hair and turned eye: those things and their predicament lowered their ranking in the captain's eyes below that of pirates and just above the black women they had, and made grounds for a good deal.

Smidmore and Everett walked back up the hill to the camp where the sealing party waited.

"Two barrels."

"Two fucking barrels!" spat Bailey.

"And three iron pots, two oars and a mainsail."

Sal gave a short, ironic laugh.

Jimmy turned and backhanded her so that her head rocked sideways. "Don't think you're worth that much, Sal. That's for all our skins."

"Do they have gunpowder?" asked Billhook.

"Yep, but they ain't parting with any."

Bailey said in his quiet voice, "How do we know this American is telling us any truth at all?"

Jimmy had already thought it out. "If he's lying and Boss turns up at King George Sound looking for us and a good market for skins, then we've got the skins on Fairy plus the skins we get at the Sound, plus we got two barrels of rum for our own trouble.

Fair enough. If he don't, we have some rum we can sell on if need be. Always said I won't work for no man again."

Jimmy told his own story of working for the whalers. That he'd come out from England on a whaler that wrecked on a reef on the north-east coast. They were marooned for two months before rescue. During that time, they caught seal and ate it raw, drawn its blood to drink. One of the men made a boat from sealskins, paddled off towards the mainland never to be seen again. After their rescue, the whaling company Jimmy the Nail had worked for started fitting a new ship and hiring crew in Hobart. The captain didn't hire Jimmy the Nail when he went asking. "Reckoned I was bad luck," he laughed. He gave up on the whaling life and went to live on Kangaroo Island. "No more working for the man."

"Organised that one well then, didn't yer," commented Bailey.

Billhook was unconcerned with the story or deals between the whalers and the sealers. His motivation for journeying to the colony was never based on commerce. But he also understood that a drop in the market for seal meant his people would not be able to buy as many guns as they needed to fight off Te Rauparaha. He walked away from the small knot of men and women, his mind worrying at the Ngati Toa invasion, at not being able to see his father's body, at his missed chance to settle Kelly in Van Diemen's Land. He was on the wrong side of the wrong country, futile and powerless.

"We'll be off to King George Sound, then?" he heard Smidmore say.

"Yep, on the morn. No need to hang around here, workin' for the Yanks. Best to be away. There'll be more people through the Sound too. We'll get back to Van Diemen's alright from there."

The sealers began breaking camp in the afternoon, pulling the shelter sails away from rough, peppermint bough frames and folding them neatly in the boat. They rolled any surplus sleeping skins around cleaned guns and into tight wads of fur and steel. They collected bladders of water from the spring. Smidmore went over the boat, checking every rope, clew and block. The sealer women gathered seed from the acacias and rushes, for they knew they may not make landfall for days and then, not for long enough to forage. They dug through the rough soil by the reedy hollow with their sharpened sticks for grubs that were tasty and fat and checked their lizard traps for the last time.

In the evening, they drank rum around the fire and ignored the carousing noises drifting across the water from the whaling ship. The women threw three of the black lizards they'd caught onto the coals, belly down. The child gasped as the lizards' carcasses stiffened in the heat and stood up as though they were about to run out of the coals, their heads moving from side to side. Jimmy snorted with laughter. "Bet she never gets sick of seeing that."

Smidmore gave Sal a flask to drink from and she and Dancer passed it between themselves. Like some of the men, both women had swollen eyes and grazes from the previous night. Sal touched Dancer's face and Billhook heard her mutter a question. Dancer shrugged and smiled ruefully, showing dark gaps where her teeth had been incised. Later, as Billhook huddled into his skins, he heard Dancer singing the chanting story that she sang often in the eve; the child and Sal patting the earth in rhythm. No one talked about the child, nor did they argue for whether or not to take her to King George Sound. Why would they? She was coming too.

PALLINUP 1826

Dancer took Weed out shooting. She walked ahead with the gun slung over her bare shoulder and Weed picked through the scrub that was so much taller and different to her own country. The small red-berried bushes looked familiar but she knew not to eat them. Dancer reefed at some reeds and examined the tubers. Weed nodded at her. Dancer broke away the roots from the foliage and stuffed them into her bag.

The sealing crew were one day's sail from King George Sound, Jimmy told them, when he put into a tiny cove at the end of a long, wild beach. The cove was harboured by a granite outcrop. Beyond the sweep of loose sand blown along the bay by the sou'-westerly, an estuary lay quiet and black among the paperbarks. While Everett and Neddy filled the water barrel from the spring, Billhook carried the net over his shoulder, corks bouncing against his bare back, and swam it out into the centre of the inlet, hoping for bream. Swans honked and took off in a flurry of black water and feathers, all red beaks and flashes of white under wing.

Dancer and Weed crossed the dunes, Dancer snatching at the reeds in the hollows as they passed. They walked over the brilliant white sand towards the peppermint forest. They arrived inside a bubble of green; a cool, scented grove, the fallen leaves making a soft, damp floor in the hollows and sprinkled with the purple flowers of a twining pea-like plant.

One of the groves smelt of roo and Dancer stopped to examine some scat. She had only shot – too small to bring down a boomer. She shrugged and looked up the hill to where the big gum trees grew. If it were anything like her home, that hill would be where the sea eagles built their eyrie, with an eye to the ocean and the inlet alike.

Dancer had shaved her head the previous night, cropping her woolly locks close to a berry fuzz but leaving a ring of hair that bounced like possum fur. Her black scalp shone through the bristles. She'd removed her wallaby frock on board and thrown it over her sleeping skins. Now her only adornments were the strings of tiny Vandiemonian shells at her throat, her belt of several layers of hair string, a powder flask, a pouch of heavy shot, a gun and her bag.

Cockatoos worked red gums in black, shrieking mobs. Dancer and Weed stopped on the edge of the forest to watch them as they ripped away grubs from shaggy bark, or clawed at the gum nuts and pulled the seeds from their casing. Dancer whispered that she had not seen so many birds like these before, and Weed nodded.

Dancer poured some shot down the barrel of the gun, tamped in a wad and primed the frizzon, closed it down. One shot, she had, before they took off. She raised the gun and sighted the densest mob of birds. The shot boomed through the trees. They saw the leaves splash with sunlight, sprayed with pellets. The birds rose in panicky clusters, shrieking into the sky. Weed cried out and Dancer stroked her head, grinning.

Three, four cockatoos flapped in the reedy undergrowth beneath the trees, their heads in the dirt; a crimson flash of striped tail feathers. Weed climbed a tree to retrieve the fifth bird. Dancer walked about the reeds, picking up the flapping birds and snapping their necks. She fumbled in her bag for her knife and cut down some vines and tied them around the birds' feet, slinging them together in one bunch.

They walked back through the still peppermint forest and over the dunes where wind whorled middens and skeletons of ancient and yesterday's feasts into busy little pockets. The birds' wings swished against Weed's side. The roar of the sea and the wind hit them at the last dune. They stopped at the spring to drink, the hard sand around the seeping water busy with the men's footprints. Weed looked at Dancer's bag. She gestured that she wanted to look inside.

Dancer smoothed the white sand to a blanket or the sheet of a sail. She put her bag down. Made from the hide of a whole kangaroo, its shoulder strap was the animal's hind legs, the body was the body of the kangaroo and the flap that covered the opening was the kangaroo's neck. Dancer had sewed the sides with the sinew from the same kangaroo's tail. It made excellent sewing, she explained to Weed in a creole of Pallawah and English, strong and easy to split into plenty of ply. Weed nodded seriously and fingered Dancer's work. Then, item by item, Dancer laid the contents of her kangaroo bag on the sand blanket.

A num's flint, a white man's flint, for lighting fires and guns. Several gnarled lumps of reed roots. Two needles made from the leg bones of tammar, flattened at one end and sharpened at the other. Dried sinews of roo tail, rolled into a neat hoop and tied off so they wouldn't unravel. Lumps of resin – tree blood. Dancer patted her stomach and rolled her eyes, showing Weed that she should eat the resin when she had a crook belly. A stone the size of a cockle shell. It was hard and pocked and lay heavy in Weed's palm. Dancer pointed to the sky. "Star," she said. Two knives. A metal knife whose blade felt like the star stone, and the knife that Dancer made herself from very hard wood, with a kangaroo's tusk embedded in gum. The tusk was filed sharp and she used it for scraping skins. She told Weed that it was a better knife than the white man's steel for scraping skins but not as good for other tasks. Two digging sticks she showed her; sharpened at one end and worn smooth and oiled by Dancer's labouring hands at the other.

Finally she brought out a possum pouch and from the furry pocket she removed three back bones; too small for a kangaroo. Dancer put the vertebrae on the possum pouch with her slender fingers, so they didn't touch the sand. Beside it, she lay her tooth, pointing to the dark gap in her mouth. Then she lay smaller bones into the soft fur, tiny vertebrae, blackened by fire. Even the child Weed could hear Dancer's heavy silence and she knew not to reach out and touch the relics.

Then Dancer began talking in her language. Knowing the child may not understand all her words, she stroked the white sand into swatches and marked it with her knuckles or finger tips as she talked. She told the little girl the story of how she came to the islands to live with the white men.

She told of the day she was stolen. When she was not really a grown woman and the worst thing she had in her life was hating her sister for her lucky betrothal to a man that Dancer loved. Her jealousy made her hateful, made her behave in a cold way to her favourite sister.

So they sat apart in the sand this day, bare bottoms chafed by middens of shell and crunchy dried kelp. They gathered the tiny shells: pointed cones and blue with the skin of the sea. Where the little mariner shells washed into the high tide eddies, beyond the black rocks where the inlet flushed out to sea; that was a good place to sit and gather and gossip and work, yes.

Babies scattered the high tide harvest with their little fists. Some of the other women chanted, sang and laughed. They picked at the shells, finding the perfect one that shone in the sun and threaded them onto stiff, dried strands of kangaroo tail sinew.

Bommies surged over submerged rocks just offshore, making white hills in the bay, and the wind was hard that day. Sheets of sand blew along the beach and stung Dancer's skin. Babies screwed the sand into their eyes and their mothers showed them how to make tears and wash them away.

Dancer's sister threaded the shells onto sinew and tried to draw Dancer's attention but the cool silence from Dancer held her away. So she kept threading, breaking tiny holes in the outer lip of the shells with a fish spine, then poking through the thread. The little shells sat at angles to each other in a neat rhythm, in and out, in and out, like the spine of a snake. The shells caught the sky and reflected the silvers and greens, an undersea journey in something the size of Dancer's little fingernail. The older women were swathed in them. Dancer and her sister had two strands each. Now Dancer wrapped another strand around her neck and tried to tie off the sinew. She asked one of the women to help her, and her sister, who wasn't asked, looked on.

After the necklaces were wound around so many necks and tied off tight, they rose and dusted the shell fragments and sand from their bodies, leaving patterned marks in their skin. Clatters of tiny sea creatures and their jetsam fell to the sand. The older women slung babies over their shoulders and inserted their chubby limbs into furry pouches. Dancer and her sister carried the bags full of shellfish. Their feet plunged into the deep, course sand. Older children struggled behind them, their hair blown into urchin spikes.

The two sisters climbed the rocks first at the headland and picked up the salt lying crystallised in small bowls of stone. Dancer's body felt scorched and fragile against the stone, after the soft sand. Her monthly bleed made her flesh tender to the hardness of the granite. They filled empty barnacles with sweet flakes of salt, put them in their bags.

The women caught up with the sisters. As they rounded the last boulder before the next beach, Dancer's sister laid her hand upon the stone, as though she were patting a beast. Dancer looked at her hand, her pink, pearly fingernails and gentle knuckle wrinkles against the orange flare of lichen. She saw the curve of her sister's breast outlined by the wild sea and her round little stomach. The nasty creature within Dancer surged again, trying to fight its way out.

Dancer saw the boat and her sister stood, stiffened and alert, but very still.

A face rubbed out Dancer's view with her huge wild eyes. Another woman cried, "Ghosts! Num!" and the little children and women were all backsides and bobbing hair as they bolted back over the rocks towards the necklace beach.

A boat. Sand, just as it was everyday but marked now by a huge creature that had dragged itself from the sea. As big as a whale but made by men. A boat. Men's footprints crawled straight from the boat to the freshwater crack in the dune. It was not good that the sisters couldn't see the men.

Dancer knew what the red men looked like. She saw some when she was younger. Their noses came first, sniffing and pointed. They looked like strange animals and their eyes had nastied when they saw Dancer's aunties. Some women went missing after that and when they returned they wouldn't speak of what had happened to them. They never spoke of what happened, but as Dancer began her bleed, one of them quietly showed her how to fill her vagina with sand to protect herself if the Ghosts ever stole her.

Dancer stayed, thinking about all this, the men, where they were. Her sister stayed because Dancer stayed. They pressed themselves into the warm wall of stone, backs against the land, looked out to see and tried not to be seen.

Dancer smelt him first. He smelled like tree fruit when the little flies came around. He rounded the corner, head down like a sniffing dog and stopped short when he saw the girls.

"Whoa!" spurted from his bristled mouth.

He reached for a strand of Dancer's sister's shells and she shrank away. He reached out again and she turned her head. Dancer could hear them all breathing above the ocean's roar. She saw that he was curious and shocked, like she'd found him squatting over a hole in the ground, that she was the one to surprise him. Hair straggled out from beneath his woollen hat and despite the heat, he wore a jerkin of seal fur and long trousers. His nose was red and deeply pocked. He breathed sourly over her. Dirt cracked in his fingers. He bared mossy teeth at her and reached for her neck.

Then Dancer's sister screamed and jumped sideways away from the stone. Her scream brought the answering calls of the women but they sounded far away now, beyond the dunes of the necklace beach. The scream brought more men from around the stone. They did not look at the sisters' faces but straight to their breasts and thighs. Some of them laughed. One man clawed at her sister's neck and pinned her to the stone. Another grabbed Dancer's arm. The burn of his skin on her flesh reminded her of her angry father when she'd run away from her new husband the first time. He'd grabbed her like that too.

She pulled against the man's grip. She knew that her indecision, her stupid moment of stillness, could cost them both their lives. There were stories of these men raping women and cutting open their bellies, spilling their insides over the sides of the boats.

The sea surged into the crevice below. Her sister gurgled and tried to breathe against the man's hand. There were six of them now. Dancer knew the men would take them. She'd wished illness and unhappiness on her own sister for her lucky betrothal to the beautiful man and now their throats were fingered by a cloud of ugly Ghosts. They were still Ghosts, even though their skins were red, underneath they were white like Ghosts. They were bloodless. All windburn and sun and underneath there was no blood.

The shells dug into the back of her neck and then clattered onto the rock. The man stood with his gang around him, her necklace in one fist. He lurched forward and took her body and lifted her onto his shoulder. She saw sky, then laughing faces, then the rock, then his back. It was the first time she ever felt her nakedness. Her head hung down. He wrapped his arms about her knees. When she hit back with her fists, another man grabbed them and tied them together with her broken necklace.

She could smell the rancid oil on the back of his shirt. Blood rushed to her face. He was carrying her across the rocks, her body flopping uselessly with every step. Someone laughed and slapped her bare skin, a stinging sound sharp in the air. They were on the beach now. Coarse grains of sand travelled through her vision. Shells. Dark, leathery coils of kelp.

A hard thump against the boat. Like stone, this wood. Dancer hurt already. Her sister landed beside her, her arms tied, her skin feeling cold despite the sun. They squirmed together in the bottom of the boat as men tied their legs together, their flesh pricked all over with salt and pain and fear.

The man who took her that day, his name was Johnny. The man who took Dancer's sister was called Cooper. They lived on different islands and Dancer never saw her sister again. After Cooper killed her sister with the gun, Johnny gave Dancer to Cooper and she had to go and live with him.

Thousands of sea miles from where Dancer was stolen, in the corner of a bay, Dancer and Weed sat still and quiet. Any language the child had learned was from Dancer's songs as she worked but Weed understood enough of what had happened from Dancer's lilting words, her movements and drawings in the white sand. The little girl crawled into Dancer's lap and Dancer held her and nodded, singing to her a long, quiet song.

Weed's skin prickled with sun shadow. Samuel Bailey was standing behind them, over them, looking down at the collection of treasures.

"Where'd you get that knife?" he asked, though he'd seen Dancer using it on the seals before.

Dancer didn't answer. Suddenly hunched and scarred, she packed away her kit carefully, in the reverse order as she'd revealed it.

"Jimmy the Nail reckons on getting to King George Sound by dawn," said Bailey. He nodded over to the boat, where Everett was stowing a barrel. Neddy threw in some banksia cones for firewood. Along the beach further, Billhook was walking with the net over one shoulder again, now gleaming with a sprinkle of struggling fish. Bailey nodded to the dead cockatoos scattered in the sand around Weed. "We'll cook up aboard tonight."

Baie des Deux Peuples 1826

They sailed along the coast by the light of the quarter moon, watching out for the white sprays lacing the reefs and islands. They passed a small island beside another long, white bay and then another craggy granite rock set into the sea. Dancer gutted the birds, split open their carcasses and laid them flesh downwards in the try-pot full of coals. The smell of roasting meat mingled with that of burning feathers and winter flowers breezing off the land.

Embers still glowed in the try-pot as the skies lightened into day. A breeze made the water black as it riffled across the water towards them, snapped taut the main and brightened the coals.

They passed through the narrow channel between Bald Island and streaked sheets of stone lying stoic to the coast's battering. As they rounded the headland and tacked to the west, the rising sun lit up a mountain scattered with massive rocks. Atop the mountain and all along the ridge, the rocks stood like silent sentinels.

"Reminds me of Salisbury," said Bailey. The sun glittered on the stones, matted over the hills of deep green and glittered again on the sea. "Like those heathen cathedrals."

Billhook strained to see across the waves. "There be safe harbour in there! Where the mountain comes down."

"Not heading into those windward rocks to find out," grunted Jimmy the Nail.

But Billhook took a bearing for himself as they sailed past the place where the hills slid down to meet its dark and secretive crevice.

The sun had only climbed a notch or so when Jimmy said, "We'll put in over there," pointing to a little cove.

"King George Sound!" shouted Neddy.

"Nah mate. Another half-day. That big bay just to the west of us is the Bay of Two Peoples."

"To the west. Bay of Two People," parroted Weed. Dancer chuckled at her, despite her dark face lined and grey from the night sail.

"Bay of Two Peoples. Two People's Place. A Yank and a Frenchman got on the grog here one night, twenty odd years ago."

At the cove they headed for, ochre stones crouched around the white sands and above the rocks, the hill glowed magenta and green with the rising sun. They reefed in the sail and rowed towards the shore. Sal stood at the bow pointing out the submerged rocks, dark, submarine shapes on the turquoise bottom, flat circles of sea above them. Jimmy steered using the sweep oar. "Hang back! Go astern! Wait for this wave," on the outside of the breakers, watching the whitewater roll in ahead of them, then, "Pull! Pull!" and the rowers pulled hard at the oars until the keel bit the sand and Sal pitched forward from her perch and tumbled into the sea.

By the time she'd found her feet and pushed to the surface, the men were in the water with her, holding the boat straight with the waves and running it into shore. Still aboard, the lurcher never took his worried eyes off his mistress. Dancer sat in state on the pile of skins with the child on her lap, both looking straight ahead to the land. The men pulled the boat in the sand until she was hard and fast and they could pull no further. Jimmy said, "It's high tide anyway. We'll just tie her off here."

Billhook stood in the lacy wash and looked around him. A small flock of white birds worked a school of fish. A sea eagle, its uptilted wings a familiar silhouette against the fat clouds, cruised high above the mob, watching. Bay of Two Peoples was now obscured from his view but beyond the headland of the cove towered a grey-green conical hill scattered with stones. Towards the peak, from one cluster of boulders, a thin line of smoke stitched itself into the sky. Their arrival had been noted.

"Have a look at this," shouted Smidmore from the rocks. He was carrying his sleeping skins, intent on finding a spot out of the sun to lie down and rest after the night's sail. He stood holding the roll of skins against his chest, looking strangely childlike for such a rough-head. He pointed to the dark hole in the hill.

It was chill inside the cave. It smelt earthy and damp but the floor was white beach sand and dry. Chambers like the hallways of the hotel Billhook had ventured into in Hobart Town meandered into darkness. He could hear a steady drip coming from one of the chambers echo around the walls. Smidmore brought in some reedy kindle and struck a light. As the fire flared, the walls glowed orange. Small circles and dots of yellow and red ochre were pasted on the walls. They looked like the canvas map Everett kept tucked in his belt. Billhook fingered one of the daubings and it crumbled under his hand and sprinkled to the floor. Other pictures were flaking away naturally as the granite shed its skin.

Neddy dragged bigger sticks and driftwood into the cave and set them upon the flames. The room filled with smoke and stung their eyes but nobody cared. It was warm now, and dry. After a wet night out on the water, their skin stretched tight with salt and fatigue, this was a "good place", as Sal had said of the Doubtfuls. Smidmore lay down his skins and settled into them. One by one, the others did the same, until the cave was ripe with the sounds of their breathing, their snores, the water dripping into a hidden, dark pool and the ever-present suck and boom of the unplumbed sea.

Billhook was awoken by Sal muttering at her dog. He rolled over to see it nudging her, a bush rat struggling between its teeth and dampened with saliva and blood. Sal tried to slap the dog away, groggy with sleep. The child sat, copying the wall's circles into the sand, humming to herself.

He climbed the stone steps out of the cave and scrambled down to the beach. Jimmy the Nail stood at the shore, silhouetted against the reddening eastern sky.

"Smoke," he said, when he heard Billhook beside him. "Yonder." He pointed to the hill where Billhook had seen the smoke when they arrived.

"Blackfellas," verified Billhook, nodding. He pointed to the headland closest to the cave where another fire burned. "That fire was not burning this morn." He looked around to the north. "Nor that one."

Everett sighed. "Ahh well, Billhook. We'll not be murdered in the night."

"No?"

"Scared of the dark."

"The Vandiemonians, yes. This mob?"

"All the same. You know the story in Van Diemen's Land? The night and day war. Lags would take a flogging rather than go into the forest during the day to cut wood. They were terrified of the blacks. Take a flogging instead, they would. Reckoned it hurt less than a spear through the guts or a waddy cracking their skull. Poor bastards; them and the shepherds. No guns and watching all day for things that moved – or didn't move. It's the ones you don't see that get ya. White folk get killed in the day time, killed or worse."

Jimmy shaded his eyes against the sky to see the northernmost smoke better. "Then the sun sets and the game changes. That's when you find whole villages of blacks huddled around their fires or sleeping in their little huts. The only way to go hunting blacks is at night. It was said to be good pickings, really good, before they got dogs. The dogs bark and wake the village up; shame."

Billhook tried to ignore the hunger stirring in his belly. "Did you ...?"

Jimmy laughed. "Getting wrecked and working the islands means I've not ventured to Van Diemen's Land to consort with soldiers and lags, Billhook. But I heard stories. Plenty. Kangaroo Island now. How do you reckon Randall got Sal?"

Billhook pictured Sal's easy smile, then was reminded of Te Rauparaha about to raid his country. "Sal does not look like a woman whose whanau is dead."

"They're still around, most of them anyway but they didn't have much choice about us taking her that night. I wouldn't be hanging around her country in the middle of the day though. No way. I'd be a pile of bones on the dunes by now."

The beach grew dark as the sun slid behind the hill.

"If we leave for the Sound tonight ..." said Billhook, "... there are some islands, yes?" He hoped that Jimmy would not take his suggestion as disorderly, was happy if Jimmy claimed it as his own.

"Oh yes. There are islands ... I say we go tonight. The wind looks good." He looked up at the long streaks of cloud that covered the first stars on the horizon. "Might be a bit different in the morn."

"Ae!" Billhook turned and shouted towards the cave. "Ae! Wake up!"

Bearded faces and then the round, berry face of Sal, appeared at the mouth of the cave.

"We're leaving tonight for King George Sound!" yelled Jimmy the Nail.

Breaksea Island 1826

The moon had set by the time the sealers sailed around the outside of Michaelmas Island and sighted another island lying behind it.

"That's it. That's Breaksea," said Jimmy the Nail.

Currents between the two islands surged and swayed but the sails sagged in dirty wind then cracked taut again as Smidmore tacked.

"A light! There is light!" Sal whispered. "Someone is on the island."

Indeed, a cooking fire burned, an orange glow on the darkened, north-facing side. Now Billhook could smell the smoke mingling with the pungent scent that he recognised as the white heath flowers.

"Blackfellas? On the island?"

"Nah," said Bailey.

They pulled down the sails, quickly trying to stifle the sound of flapping canvas. It was past midnight and whoever was on the island would no doubt be sleeping but Jimmy wanted to keep his advantage. Each man took an oar and fitted them to the rowlocks. They rowed towards the rocks, their oars dripping with shining blue phosphorescence.

Once they'd reached the island, Jimmy ordered them to row along the rocks quietly, looking for boats, ropes or gear that would identify the island's occupants. They rowed for a short while, steering clear of the sucky holes between the rocks, listening to the crying penguins. They rounded a smooth curve of streaked stone and when Billhook looked up, all he could see was the stone sweeping up to the sky full of stars.

A gunshot boomed over the water and echoed against the sheer wall of Michaelmas Island.

"Jesus!"

The boatload of women, men, children and dog, shocked from their midnight reverie, scrambled to find shelter behind the gunwales. A minute or so later, another shot cracked into the night air and pellets sprayed the water on their port side.

"Four o'clock to starboard, Jimmy," chorused Billhook and Bailey at once, when they saw the second flash of gunpowder amongst a dark jumble of boulders. The shooter had watched them pass before taking a shot. Billhook heard the clasp of his powder horn snap shut. Smidmore wriggled his fowler from its oilskin cover and loaded the gun in the dark. When he fired towards the rocks, the powder fizzed in the frizzon with a green spark and sulphur smoke and then went out. A flash in the pan. He cursed and started reloading.

"Just made us all a fucking nice target, Smidmore," muttered Jimmy.

"Who goes?" a voice from the rocks shouted across the breeze.

"Crew of the *Gov'nor Brisbane*," shouted Jimmy.

For a moment the man with the gun was silent.

Smidmore tamped another wad down and withdrew the ramrod with a steely flourish.

"Jimmy the Nail?" said the shooter.

"That'd be me."

"It's Hobby here. Hobson."

Jimmy laughed and turned the tiller back to where the shooter was spotted. "Hobson! Stop trying to kill us, you merry-begotten bastard."

Dark ghoulish shapes, attracted by gunfire, stumbled down the hill from the little cooking fire to the sea. They stood on the rocks beside Hobson. Billhook saw the outline of Mary's fuzzy halo, her plump body encased in skins; and the black jacks Simon and Hamilton standing behind her. The others, he couldn't make out in the night.

Dancer called to Mary using her native name and Mary replied in language. Hobson directed Jimmy back to the cove they had just rowed past, where the surge was at its weakest. Soon the keel of the boat bumped against submerged stones and the islanders waded out to grapple at the gunwales and hold it steady. Dancer was the first over the side, slipping on the slimy rocks and stumbling through the water to Mary, sobbing and singing a greeting and holding her old friend. The third shot, when Smidmore discharged his loaded rifle towards Michaelmas, made them both scream and clutch each other even tighter.

It was only then that Billhook noticed the two other clinkers and a jolly-boat nestled into the rocks like flotsam. Once they'd pulled their own boat out of the water and tied her off, the newcomers followed their fellow crew up the winding bird track to the camp.

Hobson's crew had followed in Jimmy's wake from the Archipelago. He said that at Investigator Island, judging by the state of the seal carcasses that lay all over the island, he must have only been ten days behind Jimmy. They'd stashed the skins – the skins they'd gleaned from the bay of islands where Boss had left them – in a rock shelter atop Investigator and kept heading west. Once Hobson had seen the carnage at Investigator, he'd decided to bypass the Doubtfuls and move straight on to King George Sound to wait for Boss Davidson and his schooner. It was a waxing quarter moon, Hobson said, when they arrived at Breaksea, and another one since, so they'd been here two months and taken four score skins.

While Dancer and Mary talked softly and the child slept huddled between Sal and the dog, the same conversation as the one between the Yankee captain and Jimmy's crew played out with Hobson and his men. Expressions of mistrust and anger clouded their faces when they learned that Boss Davidson would likely never return for them. The errant Boss was subject to similar curses and obscene titles, and then they questioned the whaler's honesty in the same manner as Bailey had.

They drank grog and talked until the early hours, until the fire burned out and no one could be bothered hunting for more wood in the scrub. They fell into exhausted, uneasy dreaming slumbers; men who knew themselves to be the only exotics on the western edge of a continent so vast it took a month to sail its breadth.

Breaksea Island 1826

Michaelmas Island rose up, implacable and green, guarded from the harsh southerly swells by the island Billhook stood upon. He could have swum the five hundred yards to Michaelmas, he mused, if he needed to. Past the island he could see the wide stretch of Nanarup Bay and to the east, the stone-speckled mountain they'd sailed past the previous morning. In the other direction, beyond the westernmost point of Breaksea, clad in lichen-stained granite, a wide sea glittering with early morning sun heaved and rolled. The Sound was fringed with low hills, hazy and blue, all the way around to the south, where the head sloped down into heavy seas. Tommy Tasman told him it was called Bald Head, and that around that windswept and roiling point, it was a half-day sail to Eclipse Island, where the seal were plentiful.

He walked back to where the two crews sat by the fire still swapping news. As well as Hobson and Tommy Tasman, there was George Thomas, Hamilton, Mary, and Black Simon living on the island. Black Simon spoke in his deep, slow voice about the American whaler that had stopped at Two Peoples and built yet another stone lookout. The captain sold them some canvas and they'd used it for their huts. The way Black Simon talked, with a thick French-Canadian accent, he sounded like an ill-born child, but Billhook knew that he was smart as a whip. His towering height, his arms like muscular, thick-boned weapons and his tree-trunk legs made for the image of a man that Black

Simon was not. He preferred the quiet life with no bother and so, if ever he spoke, his voice was soft and slow, considered.

Then Hobson mentioned the other sealing schooner that had arrived in the dead of night one month ago. The next morning, Hobson and his crew were startled to find the *Hunter* moored in the Breaksea road. The owner-operator of the schooner dropped five men and two dogs on the island with two small boats and few provisions, and left bound for Mauritius the same day.

"He had five titters and their dogs aboard the *Hunter* too: Vandiemonians," said Hobson. He scratched at a sore at the corner of his mouth and the scab came away through his beard. "Coulda been so kind to leave them with us, keep dear Mary company."

"Who was boatsteerer?" asked Jimmy the Nail.

"John Randall."

"Randall?" Jimmy laughed. "Randall. So what happened to that mob? They're not here on Breaksea are they? Shit, I'd like to see old Randall again."

"Randall's no mate of mine," grumbled Smidmore, and Jimmy laughed.

"We reckon they left for Chatham Island and the Swan River. They went around Bald Head. Took a bit of persuading ..." said Hobson.

Tommy Tasman laughed. "Persuadin'! George got himself a busted arm. One o' Randall's men, Tommy North, he got a busted eye socket. Both from swingin' oars at each other. Then Black Simon here came out with his cutlass and cut through the mob like a fuckin' orca through squid. Should have seen that Black Simon work when they got on his bad side. They got back in those boats after that and took off."

"Shouldna come here with no food nor supplies," Hobson said, defending their exiling of Jimmy's old friend. "The *Hunter* shouldna left no one here to leech off of us. This is our patch anyway. Don't need no other bastard fishing it out."

Jimmy didn't look too worried. "They'll be back sooner or later," he said.

*

Whenever it was calm enough or boredom struck them, Hobson and his crew showed Jimmy's men the lay of King George Sound and its surrounds. From their talk of the place, Billhook could see that the sealers, despite now knowing they'd been abandoned, were happier with the Sound than anywhere else they'd been. Their watering point lay in a quiet turquoise bay sheltered from the winds by granite outcrops. A stream of clear, fresh water sliced through the white sand and it was an easy task to siphon it into barrels. Hobson's crew called it Catshark Bay, after the small, striped sharks that lived in the seagrass meadows there. Through the stone-bound channel at Point Possession lay the huge, protected Princess Royal Harbour where a man could always find somewhere out of the weather. They showed the newcomers dappled, shady forests on the south side where there was timber aplenty for boat repairs and building huts, and grass trees packed with resin for caulking. At the northern boundary of the Sound was another harbour, shallower with long banks of seagrass and commonly called Oyster Harbour for all the shellfish that crowded the red rocks. In the centre of this harbour was a small island that Hobson called Green Island, dotted with pink mallows flowering against a verdant green.

Their camp on the north face of Breaksea was made of two huts, fashioned from solid timber poles they'd cut on the mainland and the whaler's canvas lashed to the poles with hemp rope. Between the two huts was the central fireplace ringed with white limestone and the shells and bones from various feasts.

King George Sound seemed to be as good a place as any to be marooned. It was a safe harbour for the big ships whose captains would normally stay several miles out to sea, wary of the winds that beat straight onto rocks. The sealers' best chance for rescue was to stay here and wait.

The women's defection from the camp happened quietly. Gradually their tools and skins moved down the hill a little way, until one night Billhook looked around and realised that they were all men sitting around the fire drinking and that he hadn't seen the women for several nights. Another fire burned and he heard the women singing quietly, or shushing Weed's occasional eruption of tears.

*

It was a bitter winter. They huddled together at night around smouldering fire with the wind at their backs. There were few seal to be found. Damp leaves stuck to their feet. Randall and Jimmy the Nail rationed the shot and powder to occasional kangaroo hunts on the mainland, meting out the powder in careful measures. The women worked harder.

Sal, Dancer, Mary, Billhook and the child took regular trips across the channel to Michaelmas Island to find food. On one of these forays they sat beneath a massive boulder at the south-eastern end, watching rain move across the Sound towards them. The women clutched at their bags of that night's meal: morsels of reed roots and shellfish. The child pulled her new cloak that Dancer had made for her tight about her shoulders.

Sitting in the boulder cave, the scent of shellfish and briny weed around him, the hammering of approaching rain drowning out the noise of the waves, Billhook listened to the women talking, and to the child who was copying their words. His gnawing hunger, the brittle cold and a kind of bewilderment reminded him of how he felt sometimes during that lean Otakau year when the people were grieving and they would not eat eel from the tapu waters.

Ae, there was no purpose in this adventure west.

As if she'd seen his thoughts spread out for her like a blanket, Sal broke away from talking with Dancer and Mary and said, "What are you doing here, Billhook?"

He was shocked away from his memory of the oily flesh of eels and all he could think to say was, "Here? We are looking for food."

The women were quiet as they waited, staring at him.

"No, no! In King George Sound. With that mob," she flicked a finger towards the sealers' camp on Breaksea Island.

"Same thing as you, Sal," he said.

She looked upset and reached out to pat his arm. "Oh … *poor* Mister Hook. Did some nasty whitefella grab you off a beach too?"

Dancer and Mary erupted. Their laughter seemed to infect the child until she was hiccupping and out of breath. Sal smacked the rock with her palm, nodding, her eyes shut, her lips splitting into a toothsome grin.

KING GEORGE SOUND 1826

They were not the only people living in the Sound.

From his favourite granite perch on the western end of Breaksea, Billhook saw the small fires that began burning daily in the hills and hollows around the Sound with the onset of spring. During their forays to the mainland, Jimmy the Nail would take a party of men to target the burnt-out swamps for kangaroos coming in to feed from the fresh new shoots. It was then that a black man would deliberately step out into clear view in their path. Sometimes painted with ochre and oil, or dusty and covered in ash from firing his country, the man would gently lay his spear on the ground when he saw the sealer's guns. There were always other men waiting, unseen. He would stand quietly. Sometimes he had a boy with him. The two parties would stare at each other in the quiet, still glades, until Bailey or Jimmy the Nail lifted his rifle. The black man would shove his wide-eyed, protesting boy sideways into the scrub, not far behind himself, and leave his spears lying on the track.

Billhook despaired at his crewmates for another opportunity lost. He was busy on the island as the evenings grew long. He carved hooks, lures and sewing awls from whalebone, polishing the barbs with the skin of the shark they'd caught at the Doubtfuls. Then one day, just as the honeyeaters were getting into the tiny red woolly bush flowers, he set off alone in the little jolly-boat, with a dilly bag of his makings instead of a gun.

He put in at the long white bay, in the corner out of the surf.

He stashed the sail and walked a mile along the beach until he could cross to where a thin plume of smoke hung above the lake behind the dunes. Here, the same man he'd seen several times before was stalking through the reeds and stopping to hold something small and solid against dry tinder. His brow was knitted in concentration or thought. When the fire took, he would step back, his face easing its stern expression and softening to approval as he watched the reeds smoulder slowly into a widening circle. The crackling and small explosions of wet wood and gum, along with the smoke, meant he did not hear or see Billhook watching him, until Billhook cleared his throat and said "K'ora!"

The black man jumped and the skin across his chest twitched. Billhook held out his hands with the bag and the man, who seemed embarrassed, had the presence of mind to look around for more sealers, or even his own countrymen who may have seen him taken unawares and laughed at him. By his side he held a smoking banksia cone and he blew on it to create sparks, for want of another gesture in his moment of discomfort.

Billhook held out his hands again and the man stepped forward, took hold of his right hand and shook it like a white man. By now, both men were surprised by one another. The black man's hand was sinewy and his glance was now strong and reckoning.

"Wiremu," said Billhook with his left hand on his breast.

"Wirddemu," said the man, rolling his r's like Billhook's own accent.

"Yalbert," he returned.

"Albert," said Billhook.

The man talked, waving his hand over to Breaksea Island and then to where he had last seen Billhook and the sealers, when he'd been firing a swamp on the western end of the harbour. He pointed to the fire he'd just started, still talking. He spoke in his own language but his message was simple. This was his patch. It was bad form for Billhook and his mates to shoot kangaroo here after he'd fired it for hunting himself. He couldn't argue with a rifle, but hunting on his land without permission made for problems between people.

Billhook nodded, a lot. Finally, when the man stopped talking, Billhook handed him his bag full of treasure. Albert sat down and spilled the contents over the ground. He fingered the whalebone shark hook and felt its barb, nodding. He examined the sinewed join between paua and wood and put it back in the bag. He took all three awls and tied the whalebone hook to his possum string belt, clucking happily. Then he handed the bag with the items he didn't want back to Billhook. He said a few words to him and jogged away down the track, the white hook bouncing against his bare thigh.

Billhook waited for a while, amongst the acrid stench of burning swamp wood, not sure of what to do, or even if the meeting had been the success he'd planned. He began the trek back to the beach, to where his boat lay in the corner by the rocks. Even if he honoured Albert's wishes and hunted for roo away from his fired country, he had no hope of persuading men the like of Bailey or Hobson to do the same. They'd already reminded him of the folly of going ashore unarmed against the blackfellas.

He was treading around the sharp, broken scallop and helmet shells on the shore, thinking about all this, when he heard a shout. Albert picked his way over the grassy dune and down to the shore where Billhook stood waiting for him. He no longer held his smouldering banksia cone but instead, a grey, furry bundle of limbs and tails. He handed it to Billhook.

Four huge eyes stared at him. Two thin white tails wrapped

themselves around his wrists. The fur was impossibly plush and smelt like rutting marsupials. As they were. It wasn't one creature but two. The black man had given him a mating pair of ringtail possums, their bodies bound tightly together with hair string, with instructions to allow them to breed on Breaksea Island.

BREAKSEA ISLAND 1826

The sealers stamped out their fires and watched the ship for a good part of the day. The man-o'-war worked with short tacks on a north wind to stand off Breaksea Island.

They looked to be waiting for favourable wind to come in, positioning themselves for an entrance into the Sound. In the afternoon the wind turned to the south-west and the ship sailed slowly between Breaksea and Bald Head, its tattered white sails vivid against the streaky bosses of granite.

On the windswept peak of the island, the sealers gathered: Jimmy the Nail, Billhook, Samuel Bailey, Neddy and Sal, Dancer and Mary, Tommy Tasman, Weed, Hobson and the others. They passed Jimmy's looking glass around and strained to see the man-o'-war's sails furled at the channel entrance to Princess Royal Harbour.

"French," said Jimmy, lowering his glass. "They're putting out an anchor on the port side. Not going to try scudding that sandbar in the harbour by the looks. Must be sixty fathoms where they are now."

"They'd be resting up for wood and water," said Bailey. "And to fix that rigging. Looks like they had a rough crossing."

In the evening the wind dropped. The sealers lit a small, furtive fire on the north side of the island and discussed their situation. There were opportunities for gunpowder and rope, items they were now in dire need of, and also a berth from the Sound to Sydney. As they talked, hope rose in each of them like reptiles feeling the first warmth of sun after sleeping season.

"Tomorrow we keep a weather eye on them," said Jimmy the Nail. "See what they're up to. You women," he nodded to Sal, Dancer and Mary, "you get some muttonbirds in the morn. They'll be wanting fresh meat. Where are those possums, Billhook?"

"Best to leave them 'til after they've kidded," said Billhook. "Plenty more then."

"Nah, they'd be worth a skerrick of powder," said Bailey.

Billhook flashed with anger. He'd worked hard for that deal. "They'd be worth more later when I'm in Port Jackson Town and you're still here looking for a feed, Bailey."

The men were quiet for a moment.

Jimmy said finally, "You're my crew, Billhook. And now that Boss Davidson is out of the show, I'll say who stays and who goes."

Billhook stood up and walked out of the camp.

My parents were proud when I was given the berth aboard the sealer, he thought. They knew it to be my future as a seafarer and adventurer. They saw me as the seed that flies through the air and travels on the water to other lands or the bird who returns with a twig in its beak so they can grow that twig into a tree. Jimmy the Nail is not my decider.

The Pākehā only want a man who can kill. They know that we Māori are brave in the face of a whale or a seal; we have no fright to come alongside and drive in the pike, hold it fast, dodge the slimy brown teeth of the bull. That's why the white men like us, for we are strong and we are brave. What they don't know is that the young men they gathered from the bays and inlets of Otakau were offered up by our families as a privilege because we have strong hearts and are sons of high birth.

Jimmy the Nail had just made it clear to him, that Billhook

was a mere minion to Boss Davidson – who was more interested in selling a ship that didn't belong to him than honouring a promise – and a sidekick to Bailey's folly with kid thievery. Bailey holding that wriggling child under his arm, Tommy and Jack standing on the white beach and waving, and Dancer's lifeless body mauled by barnacles and later by Jimmy the Nail.

At that moment on Breaksea he wanted nothing more than to be away from these useless violences. There was Captain Kelly to find and Otakau to defend. There was his father to honour. The arrival of the Frenchmen had cleared his position in his mind, the way autumn rain washes the dust haze from the horizon.

He sat on a rock that still seeped the warmth of the day's sun, above the women's camp, and looked out across the water to Michaelmas Island. Beyond the island, a swelling moon rose over a hill on the mainland. Four dark figures – three women and the child – trod silently along the path in front of him and made their way to their fire. They didn't notice him sitting there as they passed but he could smell the muttonbird oil that they had smeared on their bodies.

Sal placed more wood on the fire. Dancer and Mary pulled off their sealskin frocks. They warmed muttonbird fat in their palms and smoothed it over their breasts, stomach and thighs in long, sure strokes. Weed sat in the dirt beside the fire and watched them.

Mary spoke. "We cry on the islands. Plenty blood. Plenty cry, yes, us Tyreelore. Island wives. We cry for our families."

Dancer laid huge hands over her breasts and rubbed in glistening fat. "Plenty cry all over country," she said and then she told her story in language and Mary repeated her, translating. "Her sister ... three shepherds hanging her by her feet from a tree. Sister ... dead from a gun in her stomach. Brothers killed by guns."

"Clansmen bones on every beach."

"People getting sick inside."

"My mama's head. I found it in the hole."

"Take us little girls away to the islands and make us their wives. Call us their Worthies."

"Babies buried all over the islands."

"Fill mouth of my white man's baby with grass, bury her on the island. We cry, we cry plenty then."

Dancer and Mary kept anointing themselves with ochre and grease and saying terrible things of finding the mutilated bodies of their kin, killing the offspring from their repeated rapes, their kid siblings stolen for farmers' slaves, an old man who bled to death with stumps where his hands once were.

They stopped talking. Mary breathed in deep. Her torso gleamed as she straightened. She seemed to suck all those stories inside herself. Billhook saw her body lengthen. The short, stumpy woman was suddenly tall. Dancer stood tall also.

"Renner – Mother Brown – she made this dance for us. Devil Dance is the dance of the Tyreelore. All women like us on the islands, kept on the islands by the Ghosts. Devil makes you sing plenty and sing good."

Dancer and Mary looked across the fire to Weed.

"Devil Dance sends all your crying away. Devil Dance makes you strong again."

Sal set a rhythm with her sticks. The Pallawah women began singing. Billhook had heard the song's strains through the night air from the women's camp in the days since Mary was reunited with Dancer. But he'd not understood that it was the famous Devil Dance song. Every Straitsman he'd met spoke of this dance with lust and fright in their eyes.

Fire gleamed against their limbs and splayed fingers as the women danced. Hips forward, Dancer and Mary thumped their feet towards the flames, their hands steepled into diamonds over their wombs, chins and lips thrusting their singing up with the fire sparks that plumed into the black sky. Their shell necklaces fell back, clattering between their shoulder blades.

Weed was staring at Dancer and Mary. She seemed unable to move but her eyes were wild and her teeth shone. Sal nodded to her and Weed began patting the ground, thumping it in unison to the women's feet.

Billhook climbed off the rock as quietly as he could and followed the track back to the sealers' camp. His own problem with being dishonoured and disrespected by the likes of Jimmy the Nail and Boss Davidson now seemed a petty quarrel. Behind him, he heard laughter and a clatter of Sal's sticks as the song ended.

King George Sound 1826

They watched comings and goings from the French ship for two days. Small whaleboats beetled across the Sound to Oyster Harbour, or into Princess Royal Harbour from the channel, returning in the evenings. One tender ferried back and forth from the ship to the nearby watering point inside the channel heads.

On the evening of the third day, Jimmy, Bailey, Hobson, Smidmore, Black Simon, Hamilton, Billhook and Neddy prepared one of their boats and sailed across the Sound. They intended to arrive under the cover of darkness but the rain cleared and the moon picked up their white sails above a glittering sea. At nine o'clock they arrived in the port shadow of the ship and the sailors were waiting for them.

"Permission to board!" shouted Jimmy, and Black Simon repeated him in French.

Captain d'Urville of the *Astrolabe* must have donned his regalia to receive the visitors. His brocaded high-necked collar was brass-buttoned around his white shirt, so tightly about his throat that it resembled an armour. His florid face, resolutely pressed lips, waving red hair and snakey eyes indicated that he would give no quarter to the men whom he had doubtless already assessed as brigands. There was nothing for it but to appeal to his sympathy and his need for the brace of freshly killed muttonbirds in Billhook's hands.

"We have been shamefully treated by Captain Davidson of

the *Governor Brisbane*," said Jimmy the Nail, and went on to say how Boss had left two men at Israelite Bay and then their present group at the Archipelago and Fairy Island. They were living from their fishing and birding, having run out of gunpowder. They had no flour, rope or rum left either. The sealers were, in effect, destitute. Jimmy didn't need to embroider the truth. He told d'Urville of the meeting with the Yankee captain and the news they'd gleaned from the *Hobart Town Gazette*.

When Jimmy finished his sorry tale, d'Urville looked at the circle of eight men intently and launched into his own.

"We have had a ... a ... very bad cross from Tenerife," he said in poor English. "One hundred and eight days, half of them in terrible weather and big seas. I lost a man. Today I have discovered that, from three hundred tins of braised chicken, one hundred and forty tins are spoiled, completely putrid, and we have thrown them overboard. There are all sorts of damage to be repaired and all rigging must now be inspected. The timekeepers need regulating so that we can navigate. My men need resting. They are very tired and sore."

D'Urville sighed. His speech seemed to have annoyed and exhausted him further. To Jimmy he said, "I do wish to husband my supplies cautiously until we reach Port Jackson. In the meantime we will be anchored here for several weeks until we are refreshed and replenished, Mr Everett."

"Would you accept these birds, in return for your hospitality tonight?" Jimmy took the muttonbirds from Billhook and held the brown bundle of feathers out to d'Urville. D'Urville's nose twitched and his lips clamped even thinner. He looked quickly to the shore and Billhook followed his glance to the thin orange light of a fire behind the trees. D'Urville had some men camped there. A sail-making or coopers' workshop, perhaps.

D'Urville made up his mind quickly, calling over the cook

and nodding to him to take the birds. The cook, a short, pointy man, hurried across the deck to Jimmy the Nail, grabbed the bunch of birds by their feet and disappeared into the galley.

"Stay aboard tonight," d'Urville said to the sealers. "I would like to know things about this King George Sound. Guilbert! See that these men get some ship's biscuit and brandy. Plenty of brandy."

It was well after midnight before Jimmy and his crew turned in, climbing into empty bunks and hammocks. Above the sound of two dozen snoring, snuffling men, Billhook heard the strains of singing on the wind from the Frenchmen's shore camp, inside the channel. French lyrics wove into familiar melodies that he'd heard on ships and islands all along the Southern Ocean. Then the blackfellas replied in song, one child shrieking exuberantly above the other voices. Billhook thought their songs may come from Albert, his boy and his countrymen, singing with the sailors of the *Astrolabe*. The music faltered and ran out. Laughter. The Frenchmen began another song.

Lying in the hammock, woozy with brandy, he went over the night's talking in his mind. D'Urville seemed reluctant to trade his powder and shot, though he was stocked well enough, and offered up his men for a hunting trip within the next few days. The captain did not trust them with powder, Billhook knew this. He did not trust them at all. The captain offered the sealing crew a night aboard where he could keep an eye on them, so they did not wander ashore to invade the land party. Judging by the ship's empty bunks, half of the *Astrolabe*'s men were staying the night there.

*

"I can take three as passengers as far as Port Jackson," d'Urville said the next morning.

The sealers were shocked into silence at the implications of this unexpected offer, and Jimmy did not answer for a minute. He worked his jaw and looked at his knuckles. He looked angry at d'Urville's undermining of his boatsteerer status.

"You'll have to take all of us, or no one," he said coldly to the captain.

It was the best answer, reflected Billhook. A bluff yes, but one that would keep Jimmy's crew resined together.

D'Urville shrugged away the rebuff. "Perhaps, Mr Everett, you are hardly eager to put yourself or your men within reach of the law again?"

"I beg your pardon, Captain! We are not escaped convicts seeking refuge from the law. And any man freed after servitude to that Vandiemonian prick Governor Arthur is quick to sail far from his fresh hell. We are free seamen who have come west after seal and have since been cruelly abandoned." Jimmy the Nail took a moment to breathe and light a pipe before he stalked out of the hold and into the rain, muttering about having to justify himself to a "fucking Frenchman".

In Jimmy's absence both Hamilton and Black Simon said, "You could take me, sir."

D'Urville looked at them, quite sanguine with Jimmy's outburst. He nodded at Black Simon. "You speak Français, oui? Then you can come on as a seaman."

Black Simon and Hamilton looked pleased with this arrangement but Billhook could see that the crew were anxious for when Jimmy found out.

At dawn, the rain set in from the north again. The *Astrolabe* swung on her anchor overnight and was now backed by a second anchor on the starboard side. Shouts drifted up from the little boat that came alongside. Seamen threw down the ladder and who should climb over the line but Albert and his son. Another man called Mokare climbed aboard. Albert's long beard was caked with red ochre, he wore one of Billhook's whalebone sewing awls through his pierced septum and his teeth were brilliant with the huge smile he presented to Billhook. His son looked tired and wary and his eyes cast down as soon as he recognised Bailey and Everett from the day they'd pointed their guns at him.

Two of the officers who had rowed the father and son to the ship rushed about, finding some biscuit for them to eat, then disappeared below deck. Albert and his son sat on a comfortable bed of canvas sail, sheltered from the rain and chewed at their strange food. D'Urville and some of the other seamen stood and watched them curiously, talking among themselves about the previous night's celebrations. One of the men used pencils and paper to sketch a profile of Mokare; a fine recreation thought Billhook, looking over his shoulder.

The two officers returned with an armful each of booty for the three blackfellas. 'Australians' they called them. While the artist battled with sharp, impatient words to keep his subject still, Albert laughed with delight as the two officers loaded his lap with a steel knife, an axe, several blankets, a shirt, two pairs of trousers, a compass and a mirror.

"And our piece of biscuit," grumbled Jimmy, watching this tin-pot diplomacy, "speaks plain enough to where us English folk stand in their book, compared to the blackfellas."

KING GEORGE SOUND 1826

In the three weeks that the *Astrolabe* was moored at Point Possession, the sailors were sustained with fresh meat from the sealers. It became obvious to Billhook after an expedition with Smidmore, Sal's hunting dog and three officers, that the Frenchmen could be relied upon to waste every grain of the precious gunpowder and shot that they guarded so jealously. They crashed through the bush in heavy boots, frightening game, rather than waiting quietly for the birds or kangaroos to settle, then crashed onwards to flush out more. A huge buck stopped fifteen feet from Officer Gaimard and glared at him. The man took a shot and missed. The pellets whooped through the trees. The gun's echoes sounded long after the roo bounced away. Without their ship's biscuit, the remaining tins of unspoiled chicken and the constancy of the sealers and the blacks to trade with them, Billhook thought that the French would surely have starved to death.

But they would not give up their gunpowder and shot. The sealers had brought the Frenchmen fish, fairy penguins, possums, pigeons, marsupial rats, muttonbirds and seals. The women gathered red berries on the island and dried them in baskets, set lizard traps, dug tubers and picked samphire fruit. In return d'Urville gave them rope, tea, tobacco and rum and shook his head firmly at all requests for powder.

Of course fresh meat was not the ultimate trade. The Captain and some of his men talked often with Black Simon in their own language and, during his last days on the island before he embarked as their seaman, the big black man would recount their conversations.

"They asked me if we ever see the native women," he said. "The men are hungry for women. They say the women are never seen. The French, they sing all night with the blacks and that one Albert says 'Oh yes! Tomorrow we will show you the women,' and then in the morning the blacks are all gone. The same every day. 'Show us your women?' ... 'Oh yes, tomorrow!' the blacks say."

"They won't give them up. You just gotta take them," said Bailey, and Billhook looked sideways at him and shook his head. "Anyways, we got women. And they got the gunpowder."

*

They were all eating the women's gatherings that night. Billhook picked the oily, fishy meat from the baked carcass of a muttonbird chick and scooped out the stuffing of damper and wild celery with his fingers. He threw the bones to the dog. Before it grew too dark, he turned to his other project, weaving sleeping mats from the strap leaves of the rushes. It was a womanish task but no one else would do it. The Pallawah women were too handy with their snares, digging sticks and waddies to worry about sleeping mats. Weed helped him. She sang funny little songs and Billhook sang some back. She looked over to his hands sometimes to see how she was going.

The muttonbird mothers began to wheel in, black and angular against a pinkening sky. Suddenly thousands of birds thickened the air looking for their chicks and the noise grew – *cheep whip cheep whip cheep whip* – until the sky above the ridge was hectic with their dark, arcing forms. The penguins began then a song of a singular, whistling man in four or five notes. Venus revealed herself in the west.

"That Captain of the *Astrolabe*," Black Simon nodded his head towards where the Frenchmen were moored below Venus, "he is famous in his country for finding Venus in a field in Greece." When Black Simon spoke he was frugal with words, meting them out like precious shot. The whole camp stopped what they were doing to listen. "She was six foot tall and cool, white stone, as beautiful as the inside of a seashell. Her ears were pierced and her hair was coiled around her neck and she held an apple in her hand. He pulled her out of the earth, from a tomb."

"No wonder the officers are asking after the women," laughed Smidmore.

"He'll get no classic Greece in the Sound," said Jimmy the Nail, "just mullet and muttonbirds and blackfella women smeared with fish oil and red clay, feathers in their hair."

"Venus," said Bailey. "The oldest whore in the world. First one out at night and the last one to leave."

"Meremere, ah Meremere," sang Billhook quietly over his weaving.

"Manilyan, Manilyan, Manilyan," chanted Weedchild, who seemed to understand which star they were talking about, and then she burst into tears.

"We got Venus of Breaksea Island right here," Smidmore nodded towards the women's camp.

"Shut that kid up, Billhook," Jimmy said, irritated, and returned to the subject of women and gunpowder. "So we send Sal and the girls on a trading run."

"Yep."

*

The Captain looked over the side of the ship, wiping the remains of his muttonbird dinner from his face. What he saw made him drop his napkin.

"We have tucker for you, Captain," shouted Sal.

At the sound of her voice eight more men, some wearing hats and others bareheaded, showed their faces at the gunwale, nudging each other and staring.

It was the first time the Frenchmen had seen the three sealer women and girl child. Billhook saw how the scene would look from the decks of the *Astrolabe*. The little whaleboat was crowded with exiles of Breaksea Island. Mary, plump in her sealskin frock, black face, red knit cap with tufts of wiry hair escaping it and rows of gleaming marineer shells strung tightly around her neck; Weed, a tiny, waif-like creature in boy's trousers, her wild halo of hair buffeted by wind and salt, resembling a sea urchin; and he, Wiremu Heke, standing at the tiller, his tattoos spiralling over the belt of his canvas trousers, no shirt or shoes, beardless, wearing a slender length of green stone from his left ear and a necklace of huge white teeth; Smidmore, his ruined face, turned eye and stoved-in cheek, his long black hair not quite concealing the gold earring; Dancer, naked but for her scars and shells, her ring of furry hair framing her round glossy face; and Sal, with the skull of the child strung about her throat, her long straight hair held back with a scrap of bright woven cloth, wearing a wallaby frock, standing with one brown foot on the thwart and the toes of her other foot gripping the gunwale.

Sal held up a heavy sack dripping with blood and circled by blowflies to show the bemused sailors. From the sack, she produced a fat black skink the size of her forearm, its triangular head bashed in. "It's good!" she said.

D'Urville ogled Sal, Mary and Dancer, his thin eyes and nostrils widening. He looked over to the cook, questioning the lizards and the cook shrugged, smirking.

The Captain said little as he conducted the deal. They were given ten yards of frayed rope and some eyelets for their sails.

Tied to the rope was a scrap of parchment with two lines written in French.

They hoisted the main and sailed back to Breaksea Island. On the rocks Bailey, Hobson and Black Simon helped them haul the boat high and dry. Billhook gave the rope and the bag of trivets to Hobson. Hobson looked at the note, tore it from the rope and handed it to Black Simon, who read it slowly out loud.

"M. Simon shall bring the black lizard woman to starboard at midnight. You shall have your powder and shot."

King George Sound 1826

With fresh supplies of powder and shot, Billhook, Hobson, Jimmy the Nail and Samuel Bailey sailed to Whalers Cove. The heavy rains of the previous few days were blown away, leaving scudding clouds and flashes of sunlight. They pulled the boat onto the beach. Jimmy and Hobson agreed to head sou'-east over the hill towards the point. Billhook and Bailey walked west along the little beach, over the sheets of granite that sloped down to the sea and along the next beach to where the spring seeped out of the hill.

Billhook stopped to drink the brown water. It tasted good, if a little of the antiseptic trees that grew above. They climbed the isthmus until they could see the harbour, stepping over the short, scrubby reeds, using the plates of stone as their path. As they walked down the other side towards the karri forest, Billhook found one of the roads the blacks had made, a neat path of chopped grasses, worn with many feet. The only sound was their footfall on the slippery leaves blown down from the last northerly.

Bailey started baiting. "How did you find that Captain Cook, Billhook? Tasty?"

"Did not meet the man, Bailey."

"He musta been a tough old man, an old boiler, hey Billhook?"

A thorny branch with yellow flowers flicked past the fowler Billhook was carrying and into Bailey's face. He swore.

"Something impolite about eating your own kind," Bailey said.

"Too salty anyway. The white man's flesh is tainted."

Bailey's silence quickened around him. Sometimes Billhook watched his brooding and imagined that inside his chest, things crashed around and tore at each other like crabs in a barrel. He glanced behind him and saw Bailey's face. One day, Samuel Bailey would like to leach my body of blood, he thought. But it is not my destiny to die in this country, with its fires and pale skies and dry, prickly earth. Where would my soul go?

Suddenly, there was Woman. She stood shining and brown, naked but for the possum string wrapped around her waist. Her sister, for they had the same shaped faces, sat on the ground, her bony knees butterflied. Billhook breathed in a quick shock of delight and felt that breath course down to his loins and stall.

Her heavy hair swayed as she raised her head. She looked straight at him. She was not afraid. All was swollen silence with that stare. The clouds flew across the sky but they were in the forest now and the air was oily from the sweating trees. There was no sound in that moment, not even the alarm calls of the birds.

Her sister leapt from the ground and stood by her side.

Bailey thudded into Billhook's back, lost in his own dark meanderings. He swore again and then stared. When he spoke, his voice was rocks in a hopper.

"So this is where they hide their titters."

The skin of quiet broke and everything fell through. The young women shrieked together, an unearthly noise in that thick, still air. They ran into the forest, a splash of brown knees, feet, hands, hair. All that was left was the Frenchmen's compass, shining all moony on a flat, lichened stone, and next to it a woven bag half full of tubers. While Bailey sniffed into the deep, dappled green, Billhook weighted his pocket with the sun-warmed compass.

*

Between the two parties, they shot two kangaroos, gutting and bleeding them in the bush. They traded one of the carcasses with the cook for more brandy and rum, hanging off the *Astrolabe* while the red-faced d'Urville watched. Black Simon was already aboard the ship and the Captain seemed to want him quarantined from his crewmates. As there was only he, the Māori heathen, in the boat and three white men whose shifty, chancer eyes seemed to irritate the Captain, they were not invited to board.

As they sailed home, Billhook scooped his hand into the briny, a quick moment of grabbing the floating pumice, and then picked up the sway of the tiller again before the others noticed. Two treasures for the day.

Later when the sun hit the water low and made it bright, Weed sat next to Billhook on the rocks skirting the island. She laughed at the oystercatchers, at their red stick legs running up the granite away from each frothy surge. It was a game to her, watching them gamble every wash on the rocks.

"Tama hine," Billhook held out two clenched fists to Weed. "A gift – which hand?"

Teeth gleaming, she laid huge eyes upon his hands and chose the right one. He opened his fist and she took the pumice stone.

"Came all the way from a fire mountain," was what he had heard his mother say, "all the way across the sea to you, tama hine."

She folded the holey stone into her tiny palm. "You good, Wiremu." Her words, from over the ranges and across the plains melted into the lingo of the sealers. "Not Bailey. He no good. He call me Weed. Why?"

She could have broken Billhook in half then, this stolen child with her tammar cloak and the woollen trousers of a drowned American boy. Her smile fell away quickly and he saw her remember that day. He was not a good man, not as good as she said he was.

That night as the fires cricked and cracked and became quieter, Billhook carved she-oak into trolling lures and sealed them with grasstree resin. While he worked, he kept an ear open towards the boatsteerers, where Bailey had ventured to barter information.

"They were in the karri forest, on the south side of the harbour, up the hill from the reed swamp, a clearing ... beautiful, as beautiful as they come."

"They like tiger snakes, Bailey," said Jimmy the Nail. "You'll never see 'em in the same place twice."

"Wait 'til the Frenchmen leave," said Bailey. "We'll get them then. I'm owed a woman."

An hour before dawn, Billhook was kicked awake with a blow to his ribs and the next to his kidney as his body recoiled and rolled away from the pain. Around him he heard the grunts and thuds of flesh on flesh and then the *crack* and *thook* of wood on bone. An Aboriginal voice shouted at him. "Get up, yer useless whitefella woman. Get up and fight me!" The kicks shuddered through Billhook again and again until, in his dozy state, he woke enough to realise what was going on. He leapt to his feet. Tangled in skins and dazed, he threw his arms around in the gloom, hoping to connect his fists with his attacker.

Whoever it was stepped back and laughed and all Billhook could see of the man was his teeth. Something hard and unyielding whacked him across the side of his head and Billhook went down.

He lay on the ground not sure what had happened. Scuffles and shouts continued around the camp but Billhook was too dazed to understand. Beside him in the gloom lay Smidmore, sleeping. Billhook shook him by the shoulder but all he did was breathe a groan. Billhook's hand came away from Smidmore wet with warm blood. Down the hill, the women were screaming.

Billhook rolled over and got to his knees, put out a bare foot and tried to stand. As soon as he was upright, someone, the black man, hit him again. In the haze of sparkles at the corners of his eyes he heard Tommy Tasman and Hobson shouting.

"Randall! Where are you, ya fucking snake?"

"I'm gonna fucking kill you, Randall!"

A shot blasted through the air. Jimmy the Nail lit a brush torch from the dying embers of the fire. Billhook was on his feet and saw Hobson standing with the rifle, reloading. "They reckon we got no powder, the fuckers. I'll show them," he growled.

Jimmy prowled in a circle, holding aloft his torch. "C'mon! C'mon!"

But the attackers had left the camp as furtively as they arrived. The islanders threw some brush on the fire until the flames reached high enough to see about the camp. Smidmore was still down. Neddy sat on his haunches, rubbing his neck. Samuel Bailey wasn't to be seen.

From the women's camp they heard Sal sobbing.

"Randall's got his woman back then," said Jimmy the Nail. "Only took him a year."

"What," said Billhook. One side of his head hurt. He still didn't know what had happened.

"Randall's back," said Hobson. "He's got those two blackfellas with him. That Pigeon from Sydney and the kid from Kangaroo Island."

"Budgergorry's no countryman of mine," said Neddy, indignant. "He's from New South Wales land."

"And Tommy North and Bill Bundy," continued Hobson. "The mob that turned up here months ago, the mob from the *Hunter* that I saw off."

"What about Sal and Dancer?" said Billhook. As his mind sobered he realised the women's screams meant they were being attacked by Randall's men.

"Fuck 'em," Tommy Tasman laughed. "At least Randall's not hitting us anymore." But he looked sideways at Dancer's owner Jimmy, ready to dodge a blow from him.

"Send off that next shot, Hobson," said Jimmy the Nail. "Just to let 'em know the time."

KING GEORGE SOUND 1826

"If you don't want to kill anyone, you gotta get the blackfellas out of the camp for the night," Randall said, "You know that, Jimmy. Cleaner work that way."

*

Despite being ejected from Breaksea Island months ago, when John Randall returned to claim Sal from Smidmore, he had Jimmy the Nail's allegiance. It was Jimmy's guns that had procured Sal for Randall three years before. That night the two men had sailed from Kangaroo Island to the mainland, walked over moonlit grassy dunes and into the samphire flats of the lakes system. They stepped with stealth through the tea-tree swamps until they found the village of huts where a quiet fire was circled with men, women and children sitting on beds of dried grasses eating and talking. In the screaming chaos that followed the two men walking out of a night forest with guns, Sal's father and uncle were shot dead and a three-month-old baby burned so terribly in the fire that it did not survive.

*

By the time the sun rose and shone on Breaksea Island, Randall's men were done with the women and they walked up the track to the main camp. Bailey, holding a bloodied piece of cloth against his temple, glowered at Randall. The two black men squatted at the fire and the two white men stood behind them, watching.

Jimmy the Nail and Randall shook hands and gave each other a wry smile.

"Why didn't your dogs bark?" asked Jimmy.

"They're muzzled in the boat."

"Hit him on the other side with the ugly stick this time, Randall," Tommy North laughed, noting Smidmore's scars and turned eye.

Billhook sat Smidmore up and leaned him against the hut. Smidmore lay his head against the canvas wall and groaned again. Billhook peeled away some of the Gael's hair to look at the wound. He put his hands around Smidmore's head.

"I think your bones are not broken," he told him and set about cutting the long black hair away from the wound with his good knife.

"Not like my bleedin' face last time I was on this island," said Tommy, pointing to his left eye. "Now that was a fight."

Jimmy and Randall continued to talk in low voices. Samuel Bailey positioned himself closer so that he could hear them. Hobson, furious after his first successful eviction, stalked about with his gun. He couldn't override the authority of the two other boatsteerers when they were chatting like the old mates they were. It looked like the *Hunter* crew were here to stay until someone came to take them all off the island.

"*Hunter*'s not comin' back," said Randall. "Boss Robinson's left his crew on Rodrigues last I heard and was trying to sell the *Hunter* in Mauritius. Market's dropped. No good, these bastard nobs. Left two men on St Pauls with nay more than a knife. Blew off the island and didn't go back to supply them. No food, gunpowder. Nothin'."

"Jesus! St Pauls. That's down near the Pole."

"Yep. They'll be raving, or dead, next time a ship gets down there to carry them off."

On the boulders where the sea sucked in, Dancer, Mary and Sal squatted in the water to clean themselves.

King George Sound 1826

A still dawn the next day and the muttonbirds rose into the sky to circle the island. A living chill seeped up through the ground. The islanders gathered on the western point and watched the *Astrolabe* weigh anchor and drift slowly out of the Sound. Frenchmen lined the decks or wriggled over the newly mended rigging. The yawl sailed ahead taking soundings. No thwack of wind hitting sails, just a gentle shooing out to sea, past the smoking breakfast fires on Breaksea Island.

All of the men stood watching the *Astrolabe* leave and Billhook knew that many of them were thinking they were abandoned again. He was. It had been a slim comfort seeing the ship anchored every day for a month. It was a sorry feeling, even if he did not like the Frenchmen. Randall and Jimmy would have to keep the crew in line now that they were alone and getting hungrier. Now the *Hunter* crew was here, everyone would be hungry.

"Godspeed to Hamilton and Black Simon," said Hobson as the ship sailed by, as though the two men had just died. "They were good men."

As they watched the white sails grow smaller, Jimmy the Nail said they were camping on the mainland that night. He picked out five men: Billhook, Randall, Pigeon, Bailey and Neddy. They readied the boat and sailed from the island towards the white stretch of the bay pushed up against the mountain. They beached on a gathering swell near the channel to Oyster Harbour, where the old whalers' vegetable garden lay behind the dunes.

"Right," said Jimmy. "Neddy, find that blackfella always on at you about muttonbirding." Jimmy knew the blacks' hunger for the oily, salty muttonbird and Neddy had fished with the locals and said they asked often to be taken to Green Island to hunt them. Neddy also said they liked to spear groper and kingfish from the high rocky ledges facing away from the sun, dark water they could see into. They berleyed up the sea with smashed periwinkles and crabs and, resting on their hams, watched the water. Neddy talked of the patience and good hand of the tall, quiet Twertayan. Billhook hadn't met Twertayan but it sounded like he had mana with his people.

When Billhook gave Albert his namesake – hooks made from she-oak and resin or carved from the bones of seals and whales and deep-sea fish – Albert hadn't appreciated their use but still he unwound yards of hair string from his waist, tied it around two mating possums and gave the bundle to Billhook. Albert preferred to fish his own way, waiting with a spear or days spent building arcs of stone for trapping fish washed like spawning flotsam out of the rivers.

Neddy returned a few hours later with Twertayan, Albert and three other men, their kangaroo cloaks slung open to the warming morning. Albert wore the whalebone fishhook as a clasp for his cloak. Their hair was worn clubbed at the back of their heads, like Billhook's countrymen. Red clay caked their straight bodies. They carried sticks to hang their quarry and spears, for fish.

"How many?" Jimmy asked Neddy.

"They all want to go."

Twertayan gestured to his brothers: an older man with a long beard and intricate scar work over his chest, a small man with curled fingers, Albert and a young man about the same age as Neddy.

Jimmy pointed to the rowlocks. "Neddy and Billhook will row you," he said to the men.

Neddy and Billhook climbed into the boat after the black men. Randall stood beside Neddy as the others started pushing her out. "Neddy, Billhook. Take these men to Green Island," he lowered his voice, "and leave them there."

The sea took the boat and the two sealers began rowing hard to get it past the breakers before the next set. The black men talked to each other, happy to be heading out to hunt and shrieking when they were hit by a wave. Neddy didn't talk to them. He didn't know their language. His face was different, his straight hair and canvas clothes made him different too. As a group, the black men treated him the same as they treated all the sealers: one eye on his cutlass and the other on the opportunity.

The oars were wrapped in spirals of kangaroo skin, fastened with copper nails, to snug the rowlocks, and they creaked as Neddy and Billhook laboured out to the island. With each creak and splash, Billhook wondered about Jimmy, whose mind was always on the game and the trap.

They beached on the north side of the island where it met the deeper water and the boat crunched gently into the rocks. Twertayan tumbled over the side and the four others followed him, their spears clattering against the gunwales. They waited for Neddy and Billhook to stow the boat. Neddy hefted his oar out of the rowlock. Billhook watched him.

"Push off!" Neddy hissed at him, his eyes wide.

Billhook knew what they were about to do. He looked back to the best of the black men in King George Sound – the five strongest, the five best hunters and protectors – grinning, rubbing their thorny feet on their slim shins in anticipation of the bird hunt. Those two girls, foraging for tubers in the forest. Billhook knew all about it then. He could have stopped it but he did not.

"They do not swim, Neddy."

"Push off, Billhook. Randall tol' us so." Randall had broken Neddy's little brother's arm over his knee on Kangaroo Island.

"They do not swim!"

Neddy shoved an oar against a stone scrawled with the white markings of strange creatures and the little boat heaved away from the island. The whaleboat, with its pointed bows ahead and astern, was perfect. No going about or shoving a clumsy transom against hard water, just turn the body and row the other way fast. A quick lurch away from a cranky humpback, from swell smashing against granite, from desperate people.

Billhook tried to ignore the lamentations of the marooned men but he watched them the whole way to shore. Checking over his shoulder for bearings was his only reprieve. Five dark figures, their arms waving, silhouetted against their green and pink meadowy prison. Billhook rowed with a deadening in his stomach, that same blackness, when the only reward for his ill deed was shame clawing deep into his body.

"There is no water for them, Neddy." Billhook's concern, spoken aloud, did not unravel his guilt but made him a weaker man.

Oyster Harbour 1826

They slept on shore that night in the reeds, listening to the thumps and growls of the kangaroos in the bush at their backs. Billhook watched the little fire on the island, knowing that Albert and his countrymen would be picking at the dark flesh of muttonbirds. In the morning, the chill crept from the swamp. Dew soaked the carcass fireplace.

Randall sat, knapping dulled flint with a little hammer. It was a black art, he said, a job best left to a man with teetotaller hands and a lucky streak. He wrapped fine pieces of roo hide around the readied flints and clamped them into the cocks.

Purpose dogged the other men. Jimmy the Nail, Bailey and Pigeon stalked around the camp, their ears pricked like hungry dogs. They moved with short, urgent actions; stowing chunks of cooked roo meat, skins of water and cutlasses about their bodies. Randall sat, working on his flints and measuring out heavy shot.

"Need rope for a roo hunt," said Samuel Bailey.

Jimmy looked at Bailey. Billhook saw a glint of new respect in his slatey eyes when he smiled.

"Keep the boat stowed but ready," he said to Neddy and Billhook.

*

The day stretched away from Neddy and Billhook waiting on the beach. There was no easterly; strange, for the season was changing fast. Water glossed silver between the little beach and the island. The sun reached midday when Billhook saw the plume of smoke pour into the sky from the island, bright orange from green fuel. He could not see Albert or the other men, only their message. He walked along the beach to the channel and looked out to Breaksea Island. Hunting muttonbirds sheared the water with their wingtips, looking for sardines.

He heard the women before he saw them, a strange crying of words in a rolling water lilt filtering through the marri trees. Neddy looked at Billhook, panicked. They heard Randall's laugh, someone grunted and the woman's voice stopped.

It was her: the woman in the clearing. Her body was not gleaming now but covered in grey dust. Grey streaks of dirt and tears marked her face. French rope bound her arms to those of her sister. They were both wracked with shivers. Billhook had seen that terrible tremor of shock before. A yellow dingo clung to their legs, his ears back, tail sagging.

Billhook met her eyes. This last year of nights when he'd thrashed awake in his bed, dreaming up the velvety skin, the breathing womb of Woman ... he'd danced them into his greasy bedding, against the cool damp of harbour-side sandstone, tethered them to a tree. She saw them all. He bowed his head in hot shame.

Bailey came out of the trees with two more women, their arms also bound, their eyes flat with fear. He had a job holding the ropes and keeping a grip on his shooter. He yanked on the rope around their necks. He raised the butt of the gun to see their bodies flinch, and laughed. He dragged them over to the boat, where water eddied around the stringers. Bailey was proud, brought his catch home to gloat. It was only the second time Billhook had seen him laugh or smile.

"Billhook! One each!" Bailey nodded to the rest of the hunting party.

Billhook did not want to ship out to the island. Dread coursed through his body. He wanted to be back in that clearing, with dappled sunlight warming his face and the beautiful girl staring at him. A strange heat filled the air. He saw the sisters look at him again.

"Wiremu," Billhook pointed to himself. "My name is Wiremu Heke."

A mad thing to do. She stared. She was scared but angry too. She clutched her sister's free hand. "Moennan."

"Don't fucking talk to the merchandise." The muzzle of Bailey's gun pressed against Billhook's neck so hard he could feel it under his tongue. "I'll break your fucking neck you black bastard if you even cast an eye on my doxy." His canvas shirt ran with fishy sweat. Billhook didn't know if Bailey's gun was packed when he pushed Billhook to the ground with the muzzle, so that he fell all wrong and was pinned to the ground like an underling dog.

Neddy cried, "He alright, Bailey!"

Billhook could not see the sisters but he felt something move through the air, an imperative, a silent order. He saw Pigeon holding the sisters now that Bailey had him held down. Jimmy was struggling to get the other two women into the boat. Pigeon, he could not see Pigeon anymore. Jimmy was cursing. The women started screaming and hurling themselves against Jimmy. A splash as Jimmy floundered in the warm shallows. Bailey let the pressure off Billhook's throat.

Then Jimmy's women hurtled past his head, their feet thudding dark against the white sand. He saw her toenail, pink. They ran with their arms tied together, touching. Jimmy patted for his powder flask. He packed and tamped the flintlock with dried bark before the girls reached the marris. The sisters screamed to their two running countrywomen. They kept yelling, urging them on, despite Randall swinging the butt of his gun into one of their chins. Jimmy's hammer fell but the powder only fizzed and the marri trees folded around the escapees.

Billhook sniffed the salt sand. Jimmy the Nail walked around in a circle, swinging his rifle, head down. When Neddy had packed the boat with their sleeping skins, Pigeon and Bailey bundled the two women in and sat them atop the skins.

"Wait," said Bailey, as Jimmy started to push out the boat. "I'm sure we're long established that this titter has been owed me since Doubtful Island." He pointed to Moennan and looked meaningfully at Billhook and Jimmy the Nail. "But you should draw cuts for that one," he pointed to her sister, "before you get to Breaksea. Fair's fair. A day's work."

Jimmy and Randall nodded. "Neddy."

Neddy broke three twigs in the gathering dark. One for Jimmy, one for Randall and one for Pigeon. One woman. He broke two shorter. The women whimpered, lashed tight to the mainstay. Neddy made the sticks flush against the wrinkled curve of his thumb. He held them out to the men.

Breaksea Island 1826

On their return to Breaksea Island, Jimmy the Nail ripped down the sea eagle's nest and the skeleton tree it straddled on the highest point of the island, for firewood.

Tommy Tasman played treasurer, preparing measuring cups of American rum and French brandy and guarded the coin stash as trade for Bailey and Randall's women.

Tommy North and Hobson presented the dressed, stuffed carcasses of a mating pair of possums for dinner.

The Breaksea Islanders readied for a spree.

Breaksea Island 1826

So. So this is where the serpents lived.

They hated her, they hated her to do this to her.

Dark faces beyond the fire watched her, orange light tracing the lines of their scowls. Is this the way of the Ghosts, Moennan wondered. The taste of their fingers in her mouth, crunchy hair and red skin, holes pocking their noses, and a blue-eyed bleakness deep behind their angry jubilance. She was forced to her knees over and over by stinking hands grabbing at her hair. Stones cut her skin, grit in her teeth. No softness in this world, only sharp, hard stuff and hate. Some men laughed the whole while they raped her, some were silent and angry. One Ghost took her away from the others, pinched her again and again trying to make her scream. When she stayed silent, he did worse things to her, enough to make her cry out in pain, enough so that their laughing echoed from the camp.

Her body stopped hurting after a while. Her mind turned away, she closed myself away from the world of men. It was not the fear of a spear through her thigh for betrayal of her betrothed. It was not her shame. She sank into the feeling of the river when she was a little girl. She was in the river, just up from the stone traps where the black water pooled deep. She fell through the water and her legs and arms tangled in the gloomy embrace of a drowned tree. It was the same painful squeezing of her chest. The same honey swim, the sound of bubbles. Strange voices shouting. Then cold and numb and still she breathed not water nor air.

She wanted her skin-warm mother but not to look into her eyes. She wanted to know the little girl was not watching. This was no dream. She knew what was happening. She was drowning.

Breaksea Island 1826

Dawn. Billhook awoke fighting away visions of the sisters.

He saw the woman crawl between the sleeping bodies, down the scrubby hill, avoiding the sandy muttonbird burrows, trying to find a place without barnacles to bathe. He watched Dancer creep out of the bushes from where she'd been hiding, to follow her.

They sat, looking at the snarling suck and breath of froth over the rocks. Dancer reached to put her own softened cloak over the woman's bruised shoulders. The dingo sat next to them. The three made a dark row against the low sun, looking across the channel to the magenta glow of the sister island.

The woman, Dancer and the dog. Billhook watched as the woman spoke to Dancer. He could see it was a story from the way her arm stretched out, Dancer listening intently, the woman fanning the cloak and her long fingers pointing out a story, a journey all around the Sound. He didn't even know if she had a name for the country she lived in.

They all saw Hobson drag Moennan's sister down to the rocks. She was crying. He carried a gun. They slid together, down the steep sandy hill. Moennan's sister grabbed a bush, the one with red berries. The plant ripped out of the hill and stayed in her hand. They both went down, the roots of the bush spraying sand. Billhook saw the sister's mouth open. She was far away and her cry drifted slowly in the sharp dawn air. They stumbled together to the boat that lay on the rocks. Hobson picked up the girl with her thin legs still running and threw her aboard, so that her head flopped strangely over the thwart and her hair followed like kelp in the surge.

Moennan sat slumped. Dancer looked away.

Oyster Harbour 1826

Hobson had gone, taken the girl east to Bald Island. His crew now looked to Jimmy the Nail and Randall for leadership. Randall and Jimmy fell straight into the partnership they'd enjoyed on Kangaroo Island and set about organising their next moves.

"There's a water run to do."

"And get those blacks off the island before they swim back."

"They don't swim," said Bailey.

Billhook was standing beside Bailey. He looked at the wound on the side of his head, where Bailey's gingery hair was thinning. He must be a fast healer, thought Billhook. It was now barely more than a scratch, like he'd snagged himself on a peppermint tree.

"They may not swim but they could build a raft. We'll get them right out of the way," said Randall.

After watering at Catshark Bay, the crew caught the easterly and tacked across the Sound to Oyster Harbour. They reached the wind shadow in the channel, pulled down the sails and rowed the rest of the way to Green Island.

The black men were waiting for them, spears shipped to their sticks. Jimmy gripped his gun. "Don't give them any reach," he said. "Stand off."

"Show them the shooters," said Randall.

Neddy lurched against the gunwale as the keel hit a rock and the surging tide swung the boat around. Twertayan, Albert and the others began running over the rocks and into the water towards the boat, shouting. Bailey tamped his rifle and then raised it to his shoulder.

"If they mob us I'm shooting."

As a boy, Billhook had seen an invading chief try to walk Otakau land, bristling with feathers and power. They did that when they wanted to take over. The smell of Billhook's own Chief Korako's anger: a sweet, strange smell, like death shivering out of his body, his eyes turned orange, his face packed with fury for his enemy's insolence. Twertayan was a man like Korako in his prime. Billhook wanted his cool anger on his side, not facing him on a stony island rattling his spears.

Twertayan and his men rushed the boat. The crew fought them off with gaff hooks, oars and cutlasses. Billhook's oar thudded against Albert's waddy. They stared at each other over their weapons. His eyes, bloodshot and wide, were rimmed with dark, long lashes. Albert smelt of fish oil, his face whitened with ash.

"Manilyan! Moennan!" he spat at Billhook. Albert's betrothed had been taken to Bald Island that very morning. They must have watched the previous evening's scene on the beach. Twisted grasses sprouting perky bunches of emu feathers bound his wiry arms. There was something of the emu about Albert, his height, his heavy brow and his glare.

Neddy screamed as Twertayan's rock hit him. He dropped his gaff, crimson seeping through the fingers over his forehead.

A shot blasted. The air still, contracted.

Jimmy the Nail reloaded with buckshot and extra powder.

Twertayan was lighter than Randall and Randall pushed him off the gunwale with his oar. He stumbled back in the water, found his balance and went straight into his deadly stance, his spearing stand.

A second shot.

"Got yer," said Smidmore.

The shot spun Twertayan around. He fell forward into the water, facing the island. Blood clouded over the shining darkness of his still body and bloomed in the green water. His countrymen cried out and stood together, shocked.

Neddy pushed away from the rocks, shaking blood from his eyes.

They got the boat beyond the reach of spears, watching the current to make sure they didn't drift back in. Smidmore cleared his rifle and turned to Randall, "Well whose fucking idea was that?"

"We've gotta get them off," said Randall. "Otherwise it won't be long before one of you useless bastards get three spears put in you, next time you go to the watering point."

*

They went back to the island again an hour or so later. Albert and his men had pulled Twertayan's body from the water and laid it amongst the pink mallow flowers, his ruined chest open to the sky and surrounded with spears driven into the ground.

They were squatted, crying over his body but got to their feet as the boat approached.

Smidmore, Bailey and Jimmy stood with their rifles raised. "Don't hit any rocks this time," Jimmy said with a grin. "Tell them to get in, Neddy. You speak blackfella dontcha?"

Neddy shook his head but waved the men towards the boat and shouted in English, "No shoot! No shoot! We'll take you back!"

The men crept forwards without their spears, across the stones, and climbed into the boat. Why was it so easy? Billhook wondered. Then he saw the state of the men. Their hair, clean and daubed with red ochre on their way to the island, was now matted with grief. Two men had cutlass wounds to their throats, the bleeding staunched with mud. Even if they didn't swim, there was no wood or bark on the island to build a raft.

Neddy pushed off.

No man said a word. Jimmy the Nail raised a sail and they gathered some wind and made for the channel, towards King George Sound.

People began gathering on the wet, white sand of the mainland by the channel. Their shadows lengthened into the sea. More people came. The shadows grew until there were three dozen or more. Women, whose long, decorated breasts told their age and their rank, stood by old men with dusty knees and elbows, shining children, and young men trembling their spears. Their shadows made a deep mark of black against the white sand, standing on the tideline, their feet toeing the water. They stood absolutely still once they had reached that tideline but still more were coming from the forest to join them.

Billhook felt fear thicken the air, and the heat of the four black men. They sweated over the knives held against their bleeding throats and eyed the barrels of the rifles pointed at their families. The sealers sailed so close in that narrow channel that Billhook could see the raised flecks of flesh on the arms of the women and the lines cut straight and neat across the muscled chests of the men. Then he saw the missing tooth behind the incisor of every single woman as she opened her mouth.

It was a shattering holler, a noise that came from deep within, gathered and clotted together to make a whole sound. The sound of all those women together could put a hole in the sky, as they sang for the return of their women and men. The children began wailing.

The noise surrounded the little boat like a sea wraith. It crept into every crack and sprung every caulked leak. It stiffened the hair of every man and itched every skin. Billhook smelt that sound and saw it; a swarm of black bugs trying to feed off him.

Since the day now nine years ago when the bodies washed up in Otakau, Billhook had wanted the murderer Captain Kelly's fingers in a bag around his neck. He thought that he would find him working the Southern Ocean, but here he was in King George Sound helping the white man kill the black man. His need for revenge on Kelly had turned him into a man he could not like. Those screaming wahine told him, somewhere in their deafening cloud of sound, that he had to get Weed away from Samuel Bailey before he sold her.

And Billhook wanted the woman.

They made it through the channel with no spear in their sides but every sealer was wiping themselves, scratching their hair and trying to plug their ears against that terrible sound. They would all dream their demons that night.

BREAKSEA ISLAND 1826

"There'll be telling no bastard about shooting the blackfella," Randall spoke to the men on the rocks of Breaksea Island before they joined the rest of the sealing crews. He looked around at the bloodied men before him. Smidmore glowered back at him. "It's one thing to carry off a couple of girls, another to shoot a man dead. You think there is no law here? You think it is only blackfella law and us? There be an Englishman with the law and a noose here soon, you mark my words. Won't be long before one of you swings for some fool bashing his gums and so we'll say no more about it."

Albert and his men were pushed out of the boat on the southern side of Michaelmas Island and left to flounder ashore. Billhook could see their dark forms from where he stood on Breaksea, which also meant that the sealers' camp could be observed by the black men. Within an hour of them being on Michaelmas Island, they started a fire that took off up the green slope.

In all the wreckage of the last few days, Billhook had not seen the child. From the boats he walked along the rocks and up a track to the women's camp to seek her out. Sal looked up, startled. It was the first time Billhook had come into their domain. Mary slept in the shade of their bark shelter. Sal sat on a bed of dried grasses next to Dancer and was applying some marri resin mixture to a deep wound on Dancer's thigh. "That Pigeon," she said. "He no good."

"Are you alright?" Billhook asked her. "Where is Weed?"

"We alright," said Sal. "Child ran away when Randall came. She lucky. She was gone over the hill before I woke up to that Randall beating me."

"Over the hill?"

"She been hiding. Hiding for two days now. I saw her watching from the bush in the morning when Hobson buy that girl and take her away."

"Today?"

"Yes, Billhook."

Mary rolled towards them in her bed. "She's up near that big eagle nest in the forest." She'd been listening. She rolled over and turned her back on Billhook.

Mary probably didn't know that the eagle nest had been burnt in the fire. He waded through waist-high scrub, fell down muttonbird burrows and made his way towards the forested island valley, sharpening his eyes for a sight of the child. The jagged stump of the nest tree was on the outer reaches surrounded in soft, waving grasses.

There was little reason in crashing through the forest looking for her if she didn't want to be found. He called out a few times "Tama Hine! Weed!" and then sat next to the stump of the tree and waited. He lay down and stretched through the grass, wiping curious ants from his arms. He crooked one arm across his eyes to blot out the sun and soon he was asleep.

Billhook woke to see the little girl's face peering into his bleary eyes, the sun boring in from one side of her fuzzy head. It was a strange awakening; her peeling back his eyelids to see if he were alive. He started and she did too, leaping back and sitting in the grass, watching him warily.

"Weedchild," he said softly, once he'd recovered himself.

She dropped her head and stabbed a sharpened digging stick

into a clump of grasses. "No Weedchild. Tama Hine," she said.

She didn't have her fur cape on, only her trousers, stained with spots of dark brown.

"Where is your cloak?" he asked. "Have you been sleeping in the bush with no blanket or fire, Hine?"

She shook her head. There were many questions but he said simply, "I came to find you."

"The men came," she said. "Mister Bailey, he woke me before they came up the hill."

Billhook felt a cold, deadening in his stomach. "What did Bailey say?"

"He say ... he say, 'Come with me, Weed. We being attacked. Come with me.'"

*

Billhook stumbled through the scrub, unable to get his dark visions of the child and Bailey out of his mind.

When he reached the cairn on the plate of stone at the highest point on the island, he stood before it, dizzy with fury, and punched into the manmade pile of rocks. It didn't hurt enough. He hit them again and again until his fists were a mess of blood and gristle.

He took her in blood. He cut her with his knife so he could take her. He took her in blood.

Billhook grabbed a stone from the top of the cairn and smashed it against the sheet of granite. Sparks flew and the stone rolled, clattering down the steep, southern face of the island. He could not see it when it crashed into the sea. He threw another and another until the cairn was just a small pile of litter. Then he grabbed the green glass bottle that had been nested inside and dashed it on the rocks.

He could see the camp from where he stood amid a mess of

broken glass. Figures moved about the fireplace and the shelters. One man lolled like a seal beside the fire and Billhook guessed it was Bailey, drinking his proceeds.

An ancient manorial right.

Ae! He would kill him! Blood dripped from his hands and splashed crimson into a ring of green lichen.

Samuel Bailey had woken before anyone else the night that Randall and his men arrived. Samuel Bailey did not seem to sleep at all or if he did, he slept like a dog with one ear cocked. He was the first man alert to the wind change at Investigator Island and the only man to take advantage of Randall's chaos. Samuel Bailey had been waiting for his chance. He took the child away and raped her in the bush because Billhook and the women were busy getting bashed with oars and waddies. As the sky lightened in the east, Samuel Bailey finished with the girl. He told her to stay in the bush or he would take her again. Then he scrambled away, striking his head with a stick to make himself bleed, for effect.

Billhook crouched amongst the glass, held his fists to his face and wept. He was there for a long time until the knowledge of what he must do became clear.

Then he made his way back to talk to the child.

*

Tommy North held the Frenchman's compass and tipped it from side to side. "It's a shitty old piece. You been gammoned if you paid anything for that."

Billhook wouldn't commit to the jibe but nodded over to the hut, where Moennan sat lashed to one of the beams. "It's for the girl. I want her tonight."

Tommy looked at Bailey who was still lying by the fire, drinking from a crock.

"You haven't had a go at her yet?"

"I like to take my time."

"She be well poxed by now. A right fireship."

Billhook was silent.

"As it be," said Tommy Tasman, looking curiously at Billhook. "Tonight then."

WAYCHINICUP 1826

Hobson's little jolly-boat fidgeted against the barnacles. Billhook held the rope and waited. When Bailey was finally paralysed by liquor and the rest of the men asleep, Tama Hine crept into the camp, untied Moennan's bonds and coaxed her away.

"You brave, Tama Hine, bravest I ever seen," Billhook whispered to her when she arrived on the rocks with Moennan and the dingo. Moennan's eyes were wide and both of the girls were very frightened. He could smell the fear in their sweat.

All four of them were spooked by the silent arrival of Dancer. Billhook hadn't mentioned the night flight to the Tyreelore, not wanting to implicate them.

"I'm taking them away safe, Dancer," he said.

"So you do good work," said Dancer in perfect English. "At last Billhook, you do the good thing." And then she did something else quite out of character. She took Billhook's bandaged hands in hers and looked straight into his eyes. "You be good to those girls now."

They sailed all night to the east. The flames of burning Michaelmas Island became smaller behind them until they rounded the pocked monolith of Rock Dunder. Tama Hine clung to the gunwale, terrified by the dark sea. He could not get her to sit trim. She clutched that stone of grey pumice. It was the shape of her heel, something else he had seen her hold when she was too scared to run.

Moennan watched ahead. She held the child's hand some-times, or she ran her hands through the coarse hackles of her dog, ran her hand against his grain, ruffled up his spine and hugged him close to her.

The sky was lightening by the time he found the inlet, marked by the two stony mountains. They surfed a rush of tide through the stone-bound channel and into quiet, breathing waters, ringed with granite, flowering with orange lichen. They spread skins in the belly of a huge cave that curved into the mountain, and slept.

*

In the gloom of the cave, Billhook woke, wretched and sore, confused, with dark dreams still soaking his body. Being in the lee of the mountain meant no warning of the squall that ripped across the sky, rubbing out the sun. That brave yellow dingo whimpered and crept closer to the side of the cave with every bright flash or thump of thunder. The stone on which they lay began to run with water. Muttonbirds kept up their crying and the fairy penguins sounded like babies that would not thrive.

He looked out of the cave to the mountain above, where huge rivers rushed down the stone gullies. He knew that Bailey would find them. He peered past Moennan's matted hair, looking for the quicksilver splash of oars. He listened for the grind of a keel against granite. Then he rolled over and sought warmth in the furry bundle of Moennan, her dog and Tama Hine.

We shall live like oystercatchers, he thought. Red-eyed gamblers watching the tide surge, chancing our lives every day.

WAYCHINICUP 1826

There was a big moon and then another, her belly swelling. All the time they lived on the quiet water Moennan did not question the Māori's lack of kindness for keeping her from her people. She was glad for the peace, and frightened too, for what would happen to her on her return. Something terrible had happened to the child. Moennan saw her eyes as she saw her own and they both knew. All that time on the inlet Tama Hine was her precious baby and her friend and her sister.

At night, they fished.

She was the tallest girl, the tallest thing on the whole inlet and above her the sky blazed and the black emu stretched out her wings. Quarter moon glowed the water. She forgot her sadness, her loss and the angry tingling of her diseased sex when the little boat swished over the seagrass and she spread her toes over the nets and used the stick to push the boat into clear water again. Wiremu forced a stick into the soft sand of the shallows, moving it in a circle to ease it in, looped the cork line around the wood. The boat lurched with his weight and Moennan spooled out a ragged net while he rowed. Later, they went back to his stick.

"Feel this," he handed her the rope. She took the wet, muddy cork in her hand. She felt fish hitting the net; a sharp tug on the rope, a lighter hit from the smaller fish, a flutter as they struggled. He wriggled a big silver fish out of the net. "Hauture," said he in his countryman's language. "Skipjack of the sealers."

"Madawick," said she.

She woke early when the air was still and cold. The wind had stopped. She left her skins to squat a little way from the cave, drove a neat hole into the gritty sand with her stream. She watched the dark loom of the Māori.

"Get up Tama Hine," he shook the little girl. "See this ... something in the water." He stood right on the lacy edge of the beach and strange blue lights shot out of his toes. He waded in further and hot blue bullets fired away from his legs. She heard the girl breathe in quick. "Fire in the water, Tama Hine."

Each step in the sea as they pushed out the boat made the fire sprites flare. Every stroke of the oars made a sparkling rush of sun-diamond water in the inky inlet and then the dripping airborne oars traced arcs of wild colour in the water beside the boat. Shrimp became brilliant drawings, stars falling through the sea. Fish flew away from them leaving a comet tail of blue fire in their wake. The Māori rowed and rowed straight past the stick that held fast his net and none of the dreaming three even noticed until they were well into the centre of the inlet.

"There be no fish tonight," he said. "Net is lit up like a Chinaman's party."

Moennan could see every mesh of the net illuminated shining blue, soaring up towards Wiremu's grappling fingers. They caught a few fish, yes, some gleaming fat madawick. But the sky was pinkening and all the blue fire creatures melted back to be secrets of the inlet.

After they ate a feast, Hine and Moennan walked over the mountain to the women's place, to show Tama Hine for when she was older and betrothed. But there was a fire burning inside the great stones and so they didn't go inside. On their way back to the inlet they broke touchwood from a rotten tree and found some good grubs. She showed the child how to carry the grubs in her hair and how to peel a stick from the tree and push it into the ground nearby, so the people whose tree it was did not get angry with them.

*

Billhook waited above the carpet shark's stone grotto, throwing in the crushed pieces of crab, bits of their bright yellow bodies and black claws. He ate the claw meat raw, broke them against the rocks or crunched the shells open with his teeth and then threw in the rest, carapaces floating to the surface, the meat and guts trailing down through the water.

The wobbegong waited beneath a ledge. Billhook could see whiskers and the snout of the shark poking out. He threw in the last crab. Waited. He saw his reflection looming over the pool, his wild hair waving against the blue and the clouds. He saw himself as a shark would see him, looking up through the skin of the water to a waving sea urchin creature waiting, a wild predator, his spear a black line in the sky.

The fish inched its way out of the grotto, snapped at a piece of crab and withdrew, stirring up plumes of silt to cloud the water. Billhook waited. The striations of stone and weed became clearer as the silt settled again. Sea lettuce lined the orange stone, a neat emerald line at the high tide mark. Billhook moved so the shark could not see him and crouched over the grotto, waiting.

When the shark emerged again, he threw and felt the barb go through its hide in one sure stroke. He held fast the rope as the shaft lolled about in the water and the shark thrashed. The stingray barbs held and he jumped down into the water, stumbling over the slippery underwater stones. He hauled at the stick and dragged the wobbegong from its grotto. The shaft of his spear took on a life of its own as the shark raged. Billhook couldn't see anything in the foaming, churned-up water.

Despite his bare feet in cold water, sweat ran down his temples as he tried to slow the shark and impale it against the sandy bottom. He felt a stabbing pain in his calf. Billhook swore, in English, and reefed his knife from his belt. He could see the whiskers of the shark curling against his leg and its mean little eyes watching him and blood from the creature and from him staining the water. He couldn't stab the fish without dragging its teeth further down his own flesh. The shark let go and he pushed the spear in further, dragged the fish onto the rocks and looked at it. Its gills undulated. For a moment it lay still, its patterns in mustard and deep browns failing already in the sun. A perfect seagrass creature, thought Billhook, almost invisible hovering there on the bottom waiting for fish to swim overhead. He stabbed the knife through its head and cut through cartilage. A black rush of blood. He turned over the fish. Woman. Her claspers lying white and useless now, against her belly.

He cleaned it, slicing through the tough skin, its gizzards falling through the hole of its gut and spilling onto the rock. Sea birds began to gather. He lay the fish on its side and cut away a slab of flesh, skinning it in the next sweep of his knife. He wrapped the meat in tight parcels of shark skin and paperbark and took his catch back to the cave and the hearth.

*

Moennan and Tama Hine came back to the cave. Wiremu was cooking a fish Moennan did not like to eat. He stood, his rough face gentled by the sliding down sun. He saw the grubs and the blue flowers in her hair and he laughed and laughed. He picked a grub from her hair and ate it. Then he picked out a blue flower from her hair and ate that too.

WAYCHINICUP 1826

Moennan, Hine and Billhook had been at the inlet for two months when Billhook went diving one day, hungry for cray. He dived down a wall of stone near the inlet mouth, where the sea came in. Down past the swarms of little fish, down past a glossy kingfish. Down past towers of stone and kelp that rose as kauri pines to the mirrored surface.

His thoughts grew thinner and thinner, the deeper he dived. His thoughts were a string of singular things when he saw the crayfish, the twitching of its feelers in a hole, surrounded by silent, waving weed.

The water suddenly grew cold.

He grabbed the cray and struggled through the heavy water towards the sky, holding up the spiny creature, a strange, new fear of the deep making him kick his legs harder. The crayfish made its own wake in his hand, its waving legs collecting air and streaming it into his face.

A keel broke open the mirror skin of the sea.

Billhook burst into the world of air.

Moennan and Tama Hine. He saw them before the next wave in the channel crashed over his head. When he surfaced again, he saw the white sail of Jimmy the Nail's whaleboat and, closer, four faces in the little boat he'd stolen the night they escaped the island.

Samuel Bailey, Jimmy the Nail, Moennan and Tama Hine: the girls' dark faces thumb-smudged against a parchment sky.

WAYCHINICUP 1826

For two days Billhook walked across the hills, following the blackfella roads. He saw no one. He gave himself up to the track, wondering whose it was, passing through cosy thickets of peppermint trees that smelled of rutting kangaroos and camphor chests.

He ate berries that stained his lips red. They'd grown on Breaksea Island, and on the Bass Strait's Robbins too, he remembered now. At the saddle between the two mountains he found a fresh track that headed through a hakea forest and then south to the sea. The prickly hakeas snagged at his vest and scratched his arms, their sharp nuts opened like hungry birds ready to peck at him.

He climbed down a stone gully stoppered occasionally with rock pools, to a tiny cove. Two fins sliced through the water ahead of him, oily and languid. He watched them, looking for the tail fins of the sharks before he saw that it was a mature porpoise and her pup. She was teaching the child to hunt along the shallows. Black periwinkle buttons dotted the rocks at the tideline. The little shellfish closed their doors to him but he prised them away with the tip of his blade and worked out the meat. Put it in his mouth. Shelly grit and salty meat the size of a fingernail, with a squirt of black iodine. He had to eat plenty to fill his belly.

He headed along the rocks of the beach and towards the next headland, where the scrub was lower and looked easier going than the high ridges of the mountain with their red gum forests and hakea. He climbed up to a scarp of granite, watching the pearly clouds. Weather coming in. Crows saw off a swamp harrier, swooping and shouting at the hawk, noisy black scratches in the sky. The hawk dawdled in the crow country, insolent to the birds' territorial onslaught but moving away, moving away, until the crows were satisfied enough to return to their rooks.

And with all that sky gazing ... a tiger snake flattened its head at him and refused to move, didn't disappear into the bush but flattened its head, lying right in the place where he would have stepped next with his face turned up to the sky, to those birds and clouds. A thrill coursed through his body and the soles of his feet tingled and sent him backwards three steps until he stumbled and landed on his backside. By the time he gathered himself the snake was gone.

No heads on sticks in this country. No impaled children to face off the invading wakas. No Te Rauparaha and his mob coursing the land like meat ants to slaughter for pounamu. Just snakes and prickles and thirst. And the kid thief Samuel Bailey.

*

Some sort of summary justice must be meted by Jimmy the Nail for the theft of a woman and a boat, of that he was sure. He went over and over the confrontation he walked towards. He'd seen the things they could do. What to do. No man with Wiremu Heke's history would grovel before the likes of Samuel Bailey.

He found another blackfella road and the regular beat of his wallaby skin shoes against the worn track with its roots and twigs helped him think clearly as he walked. He reckoned on another day of walking before he made it to King George

Sound and by then his mind would be where it needed to be when he found Bailey.

No. No negotiation. He had to kill him. His crew would not bother him after that.

And Moennan. Moennan. Back at the island with all of them.

He should have killed him that day. A good part of that afternoon's work stealing women and Bailey's blood wasted, trying not to look at the man and knowing what he had done with the child. Who knew what crimes he had forced on Tama Hine by now? It had been eight hours since they sailed out of the inlet. Two days of walking and no boat to get to the islands and Bailey will have already done more damage. And sold her too.

That Bass Strait sealer, the Policeman; so he had a child bride. A black sprite with twig legs and no taller than Billhook's waist. Called himself a lawman. Negotiator, mediator, diplomat, owner of a girl he'd stolen as a baby. No pregnancies: that was what Jimmy the Nail had said, wasn't it? It's better like that. Before they bleed they can fuck and work and work and fuck and not have babies. Billhook thought about Dancer's words before her Devil Dance: babies getting grass stuffed in their mouths or given to missionaries in Launceston, taken as servants by settlers who then "set them free" in a foreign country when they got too difficult. If they were lucky, the children stayed alive on the island and worked catching muttonbird chicks for their upkeep. That island, Robbins, was seething with snakes. Snakes everywhere, going after the muttonbird eggs and chicks. Kids with their arms down muttonbird holes getting bitten. Getting whipped when they didn't want to get bitten again. They gave the women gloves but the kids had to work barehanded.

He saw a plume of smoke blowing west from the next peak and wondered at the daily talking done with spires of smoke. As he walked and watched the smoke, he felt helpless and adrift amid his thoughts of the children. Those men on Michaelmas were not so subtle with the fire that ripped up the side of the island. Talking to their whanae any way they could. Smoke. Always smoke in this country. After Kelly and his men had been through his village, burned the marae and all the houses and sawn the canoes in half, Nga Rua had smoked the old men and the crying mothers of dead sons. What leaves did she use? It had smelled lovely and clean, that smoke. Black Simon said that the Indians did that too. Not that the man had ever seen a real Red Indian with smoke and arrows. The only Indian Black Simon had seen was aboard a whaler out of Nantucket. He'd been crimped as a child by the Quakers in the middle of the Indian wars, said Black Simon. Those men who preached against war and slavery had found a berth for both Indian, and Black Simon, whose hulking frame still bore the scars of his bondage. Folk from all nations and wars, all sitting on an island now with their different scar stories, different smoke stories, abandoned by their pirate scum, Boss Davidson, waiting, waiting for something to happen.

The country changed to burnt patches of bush making his travel easier. Fresh new shoots gleamed green against the blackened earth and crimson regrowth budded from burnt branches. Christmas tree flowers flared the colour of flames. The trail was still stark through the red gum forest and Billhook's fur shoes quickly turned black with ash.

That night he set a small fire and lay down beside it on a flat face of rock. He could not remember the last time he'd lain down alone by a fire. He watched the sky darken beyond the nippled mountain, one eye level with a platoon of tiny ants cutting an ancient track across the granite. No breathing sighs, snores of fellow travellers, no shouts nor grunts or the whimpering dreams of dogs and men, no fireside songs of the women. The dusky bird melodies, the twitches and slithers seemed to conspire against him. The sea was miles away and its usually close comfort was a distant rhythm. Currawongs mocked him while alerting their mates to his presence. He heard the clicking of a possum. Red gums swished with treetop fights and romances and the ground thumped with wallabies. And somewhere, the mournful wooing of a ground frog.

Then, after a few moments of ominous creaking, a shotgun cracked through the night air. Billhook leapt to his feet and sparks exploded around his waist. He stood, bewildered for a moment, not understanding. Someone had shot at him. He dropped down, waited for the next shot.

Lying belly down on the rock, looking away from the fire to steel his night vision, he peered into the gloom of the bush. He heard a startled snake slither past him and into the grasses surrounding the stone. Felt that fright hammer at his breast again. Lizard, he consoled himself. Lizards' legs make rustling noises. Serpents are silent.

Billhook turned back to the fire, a thing that he knew on this dark night. He nearly laughed out loud when he saw the heaved up stone and caved in coals. No gunshot that bang. No one had shot at him. No, it was the fire itself, cracking the stone with its heat, breaking open the stone like an egg.

Rattled and hungry, he lay awake long after the quarter moon sank behind the land. When he slept, his dreams were infested with cold-eyed sharks. Instead of the long-fingered naiads, toothy swathes of small reef sharks hunted him in packs as he dived down through granite towers to find the two brown girls. He couldn't see Moennan and Tama Hine and he couldn't form their names in his gluey mouth to call for them. He looked into caves and the flowering grottoes of crayfish homes. The sharks nipped and harried at him as he swam. The small, triangular punctures in his hands and feet gave him no pain or sensation.

But the kelpy streams of his blood pouring up to the curve of the sea's surface terrified him and still he could not see the girls proper, only their faces gauzy in the water like wraiths, and sharks wriggling, frenzied, through the red plumes of his blood.

ECLIPSE ISLAND 1826

Bailey lowered the child on a rope, down the southern cliffs pocked with wind and sea, down to where the water boiled, and deposited her in a cradle of granite. She threw the tracer heavy with lead and abalone bait into the groper hole. Mutton birds and terns wheeled about, nearly touching her body, excited by berley and bait. The rope chafed and cut at her armpits but she didn't remove it, knowing it would save her from the sly surge of a rogue wave. She saw the big shark come out of the water below her, lift its head and watch her with one eye, slide past and return, checking her, as if she was a seal, just waiting for her to slip into the water. When she caught the groper, she knew, she saw the big blue fish eye off her crab berley and go for the chunk of abalone on the gang hook. A wash of whitewater hid the fish, slid away. She let the fish run until she felt the hook bite. She looked up to Bailey watching from high on the cliff. He put the line over his shoulder and hauled the fish out of the water. It slid over the barnacles gasping. The fish was as big as Tama Hine and deep, glossy blue with fat lips and milk teeth that looked like her own.

Bailey lurched up the hill with the groper struggling on the line behind him, laughing. He ignored the girl left alone at the bottom with the swell bashing about her feet and a rope around her chest. The blue fish slapped its tail against the top of the cliff and disappeared from sight.

She sat there for a long time. She wanted to climb but the

stone was a straight face and it meant travelling along the sucking water's edge, to where a thin crack streaked up through the granite that she could insert her fingers and toes into. Her feet tingled with fear, just looking at it. Her stomach began to growl, anxious and hungry.

Tama Hine worked for Bailey now, since Jimmy the Nail and Randall left them on the island several days ago. She was a long way from Dancer and Sal. She couldn't even see Breaksea Island from the peak of the island Bailey had taken them to. Just her and Moennan and Bailey. Bailey's first move after the other sealers sailed away was to tie Moennan's dog to a tree. A good hunter, that dog. A good birder too and warmth at night, but the first thing Bailey did was tie it up and kick it to death in front of Moennan and Tama Hine, so they could see what he could do.

Tama Hine sat for hours, thinking about the climb. When the sun began its descent to the west, Moennan's shining face appeared over the ledge, her hair wild against the updraft, smiling with relief as she clenched the stray end of the rope. "Ah Hine!" she shouted in language. "Thought you were gone, girl!"

That night, Bailey wiped his hands over the little girl's face while she lay like a corpse, cold and still. He could. He could do whatever he wanted. Tama Hine knew that. He put his hand on her bare, flat chest and felt her galloping heart. He could do whatever he wanted. Sparing her life was his only kindness.

Moennan watched Bailey with the child. He tied up Moennan every night, bound her arms with rope and kept her tied all night, so she lay hard on her side with her arms behind her. He swept back Tama Hine's hair from her face as she lay, frozen. He whispered things to her.

"You want to go home, little Elizabeth? I'll take you home. I'll get you home, Elizabeth. Give me a little kiss and I'll take you home."

Tama Hine could see the whites of Moennan's eyes in the fire's light. She nodded at Bailey. Bailey's beard scraped her face and his hot, fetid tongue was in her mouth and she felt his teeth. Then Bailey crawled across the skins to Moennan and her watching eyes became obscured by Bailey's body. The sounds of the dark sea became second to that of the grunts and moans from his chest and the fleshy thuds from his fists.

In the morning Moennan's face was bleeding and her nose was swollen. Tama Hine stared at her and went down to the north side rocks to wash herself. She scooped fresh water from the spring that seeped from under the granite and brought handfuls to her mouth.

*

Bailey roamed the island during the day, carrying with him a large stick, a knife and a bladder of the Frenchman's brandy, leaving Moennan and Hine to get his food. He started drinking more when the swell came up and they could not go out for seal. They caught muttonbird chicks, or lizards. Bailey roamed the island, not working, shouting sometimes into the wind, came back for some food. Bailey was not so frightening when he drank all day from his flask. It was easier to avoid him and when they could not, his blows failed to find purchase. Bailey did not sleep though, when he drank the brandy. The nights were long and Tama Hine and Moennan huddled together to keep away the screaming, ceaseless wind and the restless pacing of their captor. They listened to him curse and rant, stumbling over rocks in the dark, his body slump into a nearby hollow, branches cracking, and his muttering.

When Bailey was straight, he frightened Tama Hine. He'd look right through her with bleak, blue eyes, as if something else was running through his mind. Stared straight through her, always thinking what game to play.

"You're the quick one, Weed. You are clever. A herring queen, you are. Not like that dozy wench, cryin' all the time."

Tama Hine nodded quickly.

"Help me get this wood in, girl." He beckoned her down to the block where he kept his axe.

"Go on. Hold the wood for me, Weed. Don't be afraid. Hold it like this."

He placed her hands around a lump of wood with his red, freckled fingers.

She held the wood and he swung the axe. She moved both thumbs and watched the axe bite into where her thumbs were a moment before. The log cleaved in two and spilled with startled ants.

"You a brave girl, Weed. Brave." He nodded at her in approval and stumped up the hill, swinging his axe and whistling.

She was the brave one, and the lucky one too. Moennan, maybe ten summers older than she, was the one he bit and hit at night, who squirmed underneath him, a pinned skink under the skins. He didn't bite Tama Hine. Bailey bit Moennan. Touches for Moennan were not stroking or pats. Touches had to hurt her.

He hit Tama Hine when she lost the groper rig. He hauled up the rope, her head banging against the rocks on the way back up the wall. But she deserved that. She turned as the fish sped off with the line trailing along its body and looked up the rocks to see Bailey's furious face and felt the rope around her armpits tighten. He hauled her up as he would a big fish, struggling against the line. Her head hit the rocks and she tried to keep her body away from the jagged maw of stone. When she was at the top of the cliff, Bailey held the rope tight and struck her hard again and again across her face until her jaw hurt so much she couldn't open her mouth and she fell in the scrubby dirt bewildered and sobbing.

"Where are those leaves?" she asked Moennan one day after her beating.

The wind began to rise against the granite cliffs, whistling through the reeds, blowing them flat against the stone like wafting smells. "Where is the plant? We gotta be rid of this here Bailey."

Moennan knew which leaves. She'd showed them to Tama Hine when they were with Wiremu Heke at the inlet. The leaves, shaped like a woman's bosom crushed together. Three would kill a man. Tama Hine wanted to pack it into the guts of a fish and feed it to Bailey after dark, wrap the fish in bark, take out its guts and fill it with the bosom-shaped leaves. Poison him and that poisoned Bailey would kill all the big grey sharks that fed from his body.

Whenever Bailey went off on his wanderings, Tama Hine and Moennan talked about the leaves and the fish and the boat that was coming for them. They talked about what they would tell Randall and Jimmy the Nail. They began to plan their escape from the island.

Baie des deux Peuples 1827

On the second day of his journeying to King George Sound, Billhook found the cave on the beach where the crew had stopped to sleep. He lit a swatch of reeds and went inside. The child's drawings were still there, pressed into the hard, sandy floor. Billhook squatted, his thighs tingling from the day's walk, and touched the etching. Granules of sand tumbled into Tama Hine's marks.

Ae, Hine. You were here.

He stood and climbed back through the hole of the cave into the orange light of the evening. Crows cawed from the top of the hill and the honey birds harassed their neighbours over flowers or chicks. At the peak he saw the Bay of Two Peoples stretched into a long, white sickle, dotted with mounds of seagrass. He could walk at night on that beach, no matter the dark, and he would be closer then, by the morning.

Hunger harried him as he walked. His skin shoes squeaked in the soft sand, above the high tide mark, and he began marching to his breath and the thoughts tumbling through his head. Walking on the sloping soft sand was hard work after crashing through prickly hakea thickets all day. It was several hours before he reached the end of the bay.

A mushroomy scent and croaking frogs. The cool loom of paperbarks. There was no way he would venture into that tiger-snake swamp. Not in the dark. Billhook's travelsome spirit made him one who thought oceans ahead but this night he ached for his Otakau home: a place where he could creep through a swamp hunting all night and never see a serpent. A warm fire and his whānau, a woman to get him grains and lizards and always plenty of good meat to eat.

He sat on the beach and looked across the bay, chewing on the edge of his sealskin until it was loosened enough for him to suck some sustenance. No wind and the water glassed off, the moon far enough west now to let the stars shine. Beyond the mountain that pressed dark against the sky, the mountain he climbed around, there was the inlet where they had lived.

Tama Hine, Moennan and me, Wiremu Heke. Over there. That was where we lived.

He awoke before dawn, before a delicious dream was ended by the birds yelling and brightness behind his eyelids. Hungry. He rolled over on the seagrass, his swollen cock springing away from his belly. He lay looking at the brightening sky, stroked himself. Gently at first, until warmth seeped into the base of his shaft and then he chafed at himself with calloused fingers, trying to capture that smoky dream woman, she with the seashelly scent and a dirty laugh. Dream woman morphed into Dancer, oiled and gleaming by the fire, into Sal and her long hair sweeping between his thighs, into the white woman he had in Hobart Town with her muddied skirts and button eyes.

Moennan.

The rush fired from his loins, his chest and from the soles of his feet. He lay feeling his heart slow its galloping beat. Seagrass prickled against his cheek.

The sun rose and shone orange on the speckled mountain. In his mind, he asked his mother what he should do. He already knew what she would say: How dare you? She hissed at him. You just wanted the woman. Thought you could take her away for yourself. She would have been better off if you'd left her on a beach somewhere for her to go home to her people, his mother said. You saved her from no one. *No one!* You only made it worse. You are one of them. One of them, Wiremu, my son. You are no better than that Bailey.

Billhook rolled his whalebone club into his skins and slung the swag's strap over his shoulder. He turned his back on the mountain and on the Bay of Two Peoples and headed south for King George Sound.

Oyster Harbour 1827

At the French River, he followed a trail through towering red gums. Drinking from the river at one point, he tasted salt, where the waters met. He stepped across a fish trap and stared down at the young bream idling in the murky water inside the stones. The tide was too high for them to be trapped yet. But it was a triumph and a solace to his troubled stomach when a freshwater crayfish backed into the reedy snare he'd hastily woven. He ate the muddy tail raw, wary of creating smoke, and chewed the juice from its blue-black claws.

He avoided the fireplaces of others too, cutting wide arcs around sections of the river ahead when he saw wreaths of smoke curling through the trees. Once over the river he was roaming on Albert's country and there was one man he did not want to meet.

A pair of ospreys high on a gnarled limb were unworried by his presence, each gripping a flapping salmon trout in their talons, ripping out its flesh. Further along, he came across the crescent of spears stuck hard and angled into the loam, where Moennan's family ambushed the big grey kangaroos, drove them onto the sharpened pikes. By then he could smell the rotting weed of the harbour and soon he began to see seagrass in the river. He nearly stepped on a snake. They each frightened the other, as the snake tried to climb a steep, lichened granite away from the man, failed, and landed unhappily at Billhook's feet. He shrieked, shrieked like a woman, he cursed at himself; if he had been brave enough he would have clouted the creature right there, cut open its belly to check for a poisoned prey and eaten the snake. No, he just screamed, and leapt away. And as his cry fell away, he heard the gunshots.

The shots came from the direction of the harbour. He hurried along the riverbank as it widened and spilled into Oyster Harbour. Tree carcasses, washed down from storms past, littered the mouth of the river. A cloud of plovers took off as he jogged towards them. He saw the boat out by the island. A boat. And men crawling over the gunwales onto the shores of the little dome of green that was the island.

Pelicans swarmed the island, scattered into the steel-grey sky and flew as one flock over the water towards where Billhook stood. He stumbled along the rocky shore on the eastern side of the inlet. As he grew closer, he could see that the men wore shirts, hats and trousers, not the ragged skins and knitted caps of his own crewmates. New people. White-men visitors to the Sound. Men who did not know it was impossible to surprise a pelican long enough to shoot it.

The men climbed over the island to the northern side, where Twertayan's body lay. Billhook couldn't see the black man's corpse but he saw the men standing around the body, looking at it, discussing it and poking it with the barrels of their rifles.

Billhook moved away from the shore, where he made too fine a silhouette against the dull estuarine sand, and worked his way along the tree line. Soon he was opposite the island. He crouched in the bush and watched.

Four men. A British soldier, his red coat opened to expose a white shirt, wore a stiff-looking black soldier's hat. Two men in white shirts and cotton trousers, and a fourth man whose jacket displayed his status as major. All four of them carried guns, although the soldier was the only man who leaned on his stock like one made for a life of carrying rifles. They stood by the body of Twertayan for a long time. Then they walked around the rocks to the little skiff on the east shore of the island. One of the men in white shirts unfurled the sail with a quick flick of the main sheet, while the other pushed off. They sailed towards the channel at Emu Point; past the shores where two moons before, the stolen blackfellas' families stood screaming at Billhook and his crew.

Billhook continued along the shore until he arrived at the little beach of bleached white sand at the channel. The skiff was most of the way across the Sound and heading for the channel into Princess Royal Harbour. The pressure from the approaching storm began building in his ears and he could see the line of clouds coming in over the hills. He wondered at what to do. The wind blew a warm nor'-westerly from the inland but it would change soon. What to do.

At the Emu Point channel, Billhook made his choice. This was the arrival of the British that Randall had spoken of when he first smashed his way into the Breaksea Island camp. The British law that Jimmy the Nail had warned them about. They were here. The men in red coats with white crosses emblazoned across their chests. They gave Billhook a new hope of retrieving Moennan and Hine without being killed himself. It was a folly to think he could fight his way through the sealers for the women. He would go straight to the Englishmen and their soldiers.

He took off his pants and his wallaby skin shoes and rolled anything else he was carrying into his swag, strapping it tightly. He stood on the shore of the channel, watching the water. The tide was going out and a strong current surged from the Oyster Harbour into King George Sound. It meant he would have to swim diagonally and then run with the tide, so as to not get tired and drown.

He waded into the water and pushed the swag in front of him, using the bundle as a float to push against. As he went deeper the fresh water beneath the salt stung in swathes of freezing fingers that grabbed at his toes and nipples and penis. By the time he was almost halfway across the channel, crabbing through the water using one hand to paddle and the other to hold the bundle, the swag became soaked and began to sink. Here the current was at its strongest, pushing Billhook into the Sound and dragging the swag along behind him. Over the waves that sprouted against the outgoing tide, he could see the opposite shore slide by and become further from him with every stroke. The swag, he held by one strap, but it was sinking and pulling him down until finally, he had to let all of his possessions slip into the steel-grey depths of the channel.

Once his bedding, whalebone club, hat, flint and bedding had sunk away from him, it proved an easy swim ashore. He jogged along the long bay to warm himself again. He was naked now, except for his tattooed buttocks, the orca necklace and a sealskin jerkin. Despite his tired body and his hunger, he smiled as he jogged, to think of Albert again, his own attire so closely resembling that of the Australian. He felt light, lighter than he felt at sea, as unburdened as a child by the river with the girl.

All burning thighs and heaving chest, he reached the rocks at the end of the bay. He was climbing the rocks around the point when he saw Jimmy the Nail's whaleboat sliding over white waves, halfway across the Sound. Jimmy had let headsail out to port and the boat slewed down the swell, the nor'-westerly buffeting it towards the heads of the harbour. Billhook kept climbing, resolute. If British law were in the harbour, Billhook would be protected from the likes of Jimmy and Samuel Bailey, what with the tales he had to tell of murder and the theft of children.

Princess Royal Harbour 1827

The wind began to turn to the south-west. Billhook reached the point where boulders nestled into paperbark trees, their creeping, fingering roots exposed by the onshore swell. Jimmy's boat was close enough that he could see five figures, but not identify them. One of the sealers bailed rhythmically and Billhook remembered the groove wearing into the stern of the boat from its constant worrying by the bailer. Billhook always moved across rocks swiftly, and so he was standing on the sloping, barnacled Point King by the time Jimmy the Nail headed into the channel.

He watched the wind rip dark blotches on the water as it raced across the harbour. Several shouts went up just before the squall hit the boat. Pigeon loosed the headsail and canvas flapped wildly about. Smidmore reefed it in but not before he copped a metal clew on the bad side of his face. Neddy kept bailing. Jimmy the Nail struggled to trim the main and control the tiller. It was Dancer who looked over to the lee shore to where the boat was being blown, staring fearfully at the barnacles and surging waves, and then raised her face and locked eyes with Billhook.

She cried out at the same moment thunder rumbled around the hills of the harbour. In the chaos of the squall, no sealer heard her shout, "Billhook!" but he saw her mouth his name and her face break into a rare, luminous smile. Billhook held out his arm to Dancer in greeting. The air chilled suddenly and hailstones smacked onto the water around the boat, beading the surface. Billhook squatted as the force of hail hit him, and pulled his leather jerkin over his head.

The crew bowed their heads and kept working. Smidmore pulled down the main and the canvas billowed into the water. Pigeon threw an anchor as far south as he could and started fitting the oars. Fork lightning worked steadily across the harbour, stabbing into the sea, and the thunder thumped closer and closer until it was cracking above them. Billhook could only dimly see the boat now. It was cloaked in hail and spindrift and he knew that if he could see the boat clearly, they would have blown too close to the rocks to bear away.

The lightning storm roared through the harbour and was sucked through the granite heads and out into the Sound. He felt as though he'd been squatting all day, battered by hailstones, but it probably wasn't more than ten minutes. Shouts and curses bounced across the water. He couldn't see the boat through the rain that tracked the hail.

He would meet them again soon enough. Billhook's stomach churned with nerves and hunger. Jimmy's crew must be looking for supplies. It was many moons since they had tasted the Frenchmen's biscuit. He hadn't seen Bailey in the boat, Tama Hine, Moennan – where were they? He stepped around pockets of gleaming hailstones on the track, the cold cutting into his bare toes, making everything he touched sharper, harder. Prickly bushes scraped at his calves. He found a path running west, just above the reaches of granite, and jogged along.

The weather cleared and only the metallic scent of warm, wet rocks and a tingling buzz remained of the lightning storm. Steam rose from the track and hailstones melted. Around the next corner, he saw the ship, a twin-masted brig, her spars wrapped in sail, swinging on her anchor a few hundred yards from the shore. A small boat moved away from the ship.

Billhook hurried along. He wanted to get to the shore camp before Jimmy the Nail. He felt his nakedness and flushed at the memory of scratchy seagrass against his skin that morning at Two Peoples Bay. If he knew there were no white women at the shore camp to shriek at his naked heathen self emerging from the forest, he would feel more at ease. A soldier bent on avenging a sweetheart's modesty by way of his gun. A Vandiemonian lag ready to mete out authority on any man lower than himself. A lieutenant with brass buttons and jingling handcuffs. Just no white women.

At the peak of his worrying at his lack of dress he saw the trousers draped across a large boulder on the beach, as though their inhabitant had lain down for a sleep in the sun, and disappeared into his own dreams. Billhook scurried down the path and looked around. No footprints, only the white sand scoured by hail and rain. He trudged across the beach to the single boulder and picked up the wet canvas. They were torn about the waist, perhaps even cut with a knife. Dark stains of blood flowered around the jagged edges of the cloth. Billhook tore away the trousers' cuffs to make a crude belt, shook out the sand and then donned the wet, bloodied pants.

He ran along the beach and over the next outcrop of rocks until he could see the tender boat land. The boat bit into the sand and two men leapt out, carrying long sticks. They hauled two sheep from the boat and untied their legs, using the sticks to fend them along the shore. The beach smelled the same, the fuggy smell of low tide and rotting weed, the wind full of rain that swept over the blinding white of the sand dunes on the hills opposite the harbour. Everything else had changed from the last time he had been in this place. Two cannons crouched just above the beach, their barrels pointing to sea, and a flagstaff lofted a fluttering rag of the British Empire. The shouts of the herders floated along the beach towards him, then the thwack of their sticks against wool, a grunt from one of the sheep.

Billhook headed for the lone man tying off the boat to a craggy paperbark tree on the shore. He looked up, surprised, when Billhook greeted him, and brushed the tree's flowers from his hair.

"Well, you're a sight then," the man straightened to just over five foot, looked closer at Billhook. "What heathen hole did you spring from? Not a blackfella, are you then?"

"Billhook," he shocked himself by saying his name out loud. He had not heard his own voice in several days. Images of the times he had introduced himself on a beach filled his mind. Albert. Moennan. "My name is Billhook."

"Pleased, I'm sure Mister Hook. I'm Mister Jimmy McCone, pilot of this establishment." He mistook Billhook's questioning look. "That is, I look after the boat side of affairs."

"What is the … establishment?" Billhook tried out the word. "English?" He scratched at his groin where his sandy new trousers chafed.

"We just took New Holland for the King," McCone said, his shoulders squaring and pride gleaming in his blue eyes. Then he checked Billhook's scratching and his eyes widened, until Billhook could see his reddened veins streaking from his lashes, and his pride fell away to dismay. He stepped back. "Christ, lad! What kind of cannibal wears the pants of a man speared by blackfellas?"

"Hmm?"

"Where did you get those trousers?"

Billhook, bewildered by his offending pants, said. "On the

beach … I had no clothes."

"They cut them away from the blacksmith Dineen only yesterday, Mr Hook. To be sure."

"What happened?"

"Them navvies went out to one of the islands and took four blackfellas off who reckoned they been stuck there. They got off the boat wanting to kill a white man. Any white man. The blacksmith were the first one who didn't have no shooter. Stuck three spears into him." McCone warmed to his subject, speaking faster as he became excited. "Before they was rescued, the blackfellas around here were happy and talking. The Major gave them some axes and shook their hands. Then he had to send out Festing to get those ones off the island and sweetness all turned to shit. Those blackfellas they rescued off the island were pretty angry. They didn't care who they struck, see. The Major wouldn't even let the regiment answer with their rifles. 'No retribution!' he said. 'But keep at least one barrel loaded at all times, to be sure.'"

McCone lowered his voice. "The attackers buggered off and the Major couldn't find what it was they were angry about. Dineen was carted back to the doctor in a wheelbarrow, all white and shaking he was, with broken off spears still sticking out of him. But one of the soldiers who went out with the Major this morning told me they saw a dead blackfella on another island. Said his legs and arms was dried up in the sun like jerky. The Major is saying that sealers have done some bad work in these parts."

"I must speak with the Major about the dead man," said Billhook. "Is he ashore?"

A soldier stumped over the grassy knoll, sighted Billhook talking to McCone and fixed his gun.

"Convict McCone! You be afforded the pleasure of a decent

flogging if you stand about. Get those stores up to the hut."

His prestige as pilot shattered, McCone shrugged at Billhook and used what he had. "I have encountered a heathen, Corporal Shore. Mr Hook swears he has news of the dead man. He wants to speak with the Major."

"Fine irony that, a Galway thief calling other men heathens." The soldier looked closely at Billhook. "Though I'd wager, Mr Hook, that you have the stink of a sealer about you. Come this way. You shall have your audience with the Major as soon as he is finished his work. McCone – that flour keg – and quick about it."

The foot soldier led Billhook past the cannon and the flagstaff, up through the beach reeds where a thin track had already been trampled by sheep, pigs and men. McCone laboured over the keg behind them, muttering that Britons didn't know their County Mayo from their Galway. They walked into a clearing where the place was changed from the last time Billhook was there, by two huts of wood, bark and thatched with reeds, several white canvas tents and rough yards for the stock. The two sheep had already been hobbled.

A convict stood with his arms tied around the warty trunk of a gum tree. In a strange embrace, his cheek was pressed to the peeling bark as though the tree were his lover. Two steps away, the Major had stripped away his jacket as his efforts in flogging the man was making him hot. Sweat ran from his forehead, through his sideburns and dripped from his florid jowls. Beside him, the surgeon checked for broken skin and counted out the strokes on slim fingers, a small smile on his pinched face.

"No man would flog Ryan: not soldier, navvy nor convict. Private Dickens said no. He'll be sent away for that," whispered McCone to Billhook, as he rolled his barrel alongside. "So the Major said he'd do 'im himself."

"What did the man do?"

"Started trouble about the meat rations. See, there is only food in the settlement for one month."

Billhook grunted and smiled, thinking about red berries, seal meat, fish and muttonbirds, and of the island pelicans who flew away from futile English rifles. He watched the Major shake out his lash for another go at the man.

Thwack. "Sixteen, sir," said the surgeon.

It was a dull kind of beating, thought Billhook. The soldiers were trying to ignore it, stifling yawns. The convicts were forced by the overseers to stand in a row behind the heaving shoulders of the Major and not turn away their heads. Only the surgeon watched with any interest. Billhook wondered at the bone-hard form of this white man's punishment, this banal exercise of power and demonstration, so different from the chaotic bloodspilling that happened in his own world of islands and boats.

"Twenty-five, sir."

"I trust you will cease questioning my authority, John Ryan," said the Major to the convict's welted, reddened back as he threw down the lash. He nodded to the overseer. "You are hereby on half flour and beef for a week. Back on full rations in seven days, pending your good behaviour." He looked disgusted with his work but he did not spit.

The overseer untied the convict from the tree, who shook the tension out of his arms, turned around and flicked shanks of black hair from his face. "You are most welcome, Major," he said in an American accent, and looked his flogger straight in the eyes. The Major held his stare.

McCone sucked breath in through pursed lips. "He'd not want to make trouble for us all, that John Ryan." Billhook looked at him. "I have been on Maria Island in my recent past and this place is a heaven compared."

Clouds cleared away from the sun and the damp earth steamed. The garrison relaxed their shoulders after standing to attention during the flogging and began to move about. Prisoners wandered away to their work. Someone called for dinner. Corporal Shore spoke to the Major, who was shrugging into his coat, and nodded towards Billhook. As the Major raised his eyes to the sealer, another man in naval costume walked over the knoll from the sea and called the Major aside.

His words "sealers", "boat", "during the storm", "native women" floated across the muddy, trampled ground to Billhook. He wanted to hear more. Jimmy the Nail must have spoken to someone aboard the brig. Asking for rations no doubt. Offering up Dancer and Sal for flour even.

Again, the Major looked at Billhook. He waved him over.

The Major smelled like salted pork and sweat. Although he had not broken the prisoner's skin during the flogging, his fingers were spattered with blood. He held Billhook with blue eyes so clear and knowing, that after watching the prisoner's punishment and challenge, Billhook struggled to maintain his gaze. His shame surprised him. He could see the right and the power in the man; that the Major was happiest being in control of other men. But his wasn't the look of a tyrant. His entitlement as leader was earned by steady, clever labour and by knowing when to beat a man and when to be kind.

"William Hook, I have word that your friends are aboard the *Amity* requesting victuals."

"My friends," Billhook repeated. "Victuals." He was hungry and the words he had been planning since he saw the Englishmen on Green Island ran away from his mind, not to be found.

"They tell the lieutenant that they are crew from the *Governor Brisbane* and the *Hunter* and that they have been cruelly abandoned by their masters for up to eighteen months now."

Billhook nodded. The Major continued. "Are you associated with these men?"

"I have been so, sir, though I am now cast out from them."

The Major considered this piece of information, his chin and eyes turning to one side. "Mmm. I have given orders for your crew to be kept aboard the *Amity* tonight. In the morning I will conduct interviews." The Major sighed. "One of our best men was speared by the natives yesterday. The blacksmith."

"By the men on Michaelmas?"

"You know of the natives who were left on Michaelmas Island?"

"I do."

"You have much to tell me."

"Yes, sir."

Billhook breathed in and with a ragged voice, told the Major of his concern for Moennan and Tama Hine. "Returning the girl Moennan to her people will make the blackfellas pleased with you," he said. "You could do that, sir."

The Major looked intently at Billhook. "The women who presented today were from Van Diemen's Land, not King George Sound."

"Sir, three are from this coast. Two were carried off when we marooned the black men on the island."

"And were you present during the killing of the native on Green Island?"

"Yes, sir. I know who shot him, sir."

"William Hook, you will provide a statement to me naming this man and the events on Green Island in the morning."

"Yes sir."

"Is this murderer one of the men who came into the harbour during the storm today?"

"I do not know sir." Billhook fingered an orca tooth at his

throat. His belly grumbled. After the intense exchange of information, he became aware again of the strange people, animals and labour around him. The order of things was about to change, he thought. He didn't like it. But he understood it. He laid out his mistruth to the Major in his most careful English. "He is the same man who took Tama Hine and Moennan away. His name is Samuel Bailey."

PRINCESS ROYAL HARBOUR 1827

He woke in the bottom of the navvy's jolly-boat, wrapped in a sail. Something stabbed at his ribs, and then again. He grunted away from the pain and shut his eyes but the poking continued. What was this? This sharp shunting at him?

In the gloomy sky, he saw the outline of a man, leaning over the boat.

"Smidmore. Stop. Stop it, man."

Trying to sit up, he remembered the tousle-headed lieutenant handcuffing him to a shackle on the boat, before tucking him in to his sail. He wrenched at his chain in frustration.

"Thought I saw you on the rocks yesterday," said Smidmore. Water dripped from his long hair and onto Billhook's chest. "Right before I fetched that tack in my eye. Dancer, I reckon she saw you too. What you doing here?"

"Where are the girls?"

"Sal's gone with Randall to the Swan River, looking for seal." Smidmore was heavy on Randall's name. He still smarted from his loss of Sal. "Mary is out on Breaksea."

Billhook wriggled upright and wiped aside the canvas. His back ached from the boat's ribs. "No. Where is the kid?"

"Oh!" Smidmore laughed, nastily. "Of course. The kid."

"Where is she, Smidmore?"

"She ain't with us."

"Where is Tama Hine?"

Smidmore leaned in to stare close at Billhook. "I should kill

194

you now, you fucking black traitor. While I got the chance."

"I took the girls to keep Bailey off them."

"I have no quarrel with you there, Billhook. Even pinching the boat. Everyone for themselves. Nah, the story you been giving to that Major nob about the blackfella on Green Island. You told him I shot the man dead."

"No."

"The lieutenant came aboard and said we was to give statements today. That they knew about the shooting. They took our guns. Six guns they got. And our boat. I'll swing for that killing, Billhook."

"No white man ever swung for shooting a blackfella."

"Makes it a better reason to finish you off now. I'll not be going back to captivity, nor threats of the rope, Billhook. I be going back to Kangaroo Island. I'll take you and this little boat, right here and now."

"I said Bailey did it. I said Bailey shot the blackfella."

Smidmore began to laugh quietly, as the sky was lightening in the east and he didn't want to be heard by stirring soldiers. "Bailey."

"Where are the girls?"

Smidmore pushed himself away from Billhook and the gunwales of the boat. He turned and walked back into the water, wading through the shallows. Just as he began to despair of an answer, Billhook heard the sealer mutter, "Bailey's got them on Eclipse Island."

Princess Royal Harbour 1827

From early in the morning, people from the country surrounding King George Sound began arriving at the English garrison. First came two young men, their chests and arms painted. Then three older men and some boy children dressed in small cloaks. As the shadows began to shorten, one of the boys left and returned with three elderly women, one of whom walked with the aid of a stick. The two other women helped her when she failed. Billhook watched her fold her legs and sink down onto a kangaroo skin prepared for her. Powerful old kui, that one, he thought. The warriors had decreed the scene safe enough for her to attend. The shape of her face traced echoes of Moennan and he wondered if she was Moennan's grandmother.

All day they waited. Occasionally one of the men would groan with impatience and leave the garrison. The old women and a boy sat under a tree, looking glummer as the sun climbed the sky. The Major busied himself with domestic matters: transcribing Billhook's statement of the killing in his tent, occasionally coming out to clarify something with Billhook, or inspect the construction of the livestock yards. Major was as impatient and nervy as the countrymen and women. He needed this day to go well.

Pigeon was shipped to shore from the brig, where the other sealers were still being held.

"Major Boss wants me to talk to these blackfellas here," he

told Billhook, looking proud of his new role as negotiator. "Keep 'em happy, you know."

Billhook shook his head and walked away, remembering Pigeon's gleeful face as he dragged a teary Moennan out of the bush. Something dark in him hoped the old kui would recognise Pigeon. But the old people would get no justice from this sorry tale and as the day wore on, he became afraid that they would not even get their countrywoman back.

As the sun started its decline into the western coast hills, a great shout went up. The countrymen had been watching the channel and they were first to see Lieutenant Festing's skiff sail into the harbour. The Major quickly told Pigeon to explain to them what was going to happen. If she was in the boat, the Major would personally walk her to her family and present her, he said. He directed Pigeon to stay with them and comfort them until she arrived at the garrison.

"You, William Hook, you stay here with Corporal Shore."

He spoke to the other soldiers in hushed tones, so that Billhook couldn't hear his words. The Major must want a show here, he thought, a show of English power. No more blacksmith ambushes.

The Major paced back and forth, waiting for the boat. He snapped at the surgeon who hovered about him like a terrier. Then he walked down to the shore. The soldiers followed, some hastily donning their red jackets, others checking their guns.

Billhook could see the skiff's sails being lowered and the men fitting oars to crab into shore. Then his view was ruined by a dozen privates crowding the boat. He saw one man lift out a ragged bundle and walk to the shore. Another man carried a larger cargo ashore. At the garrison, the mood intensified. The kui talked quickly, her words pitching into short wails. A countryman patted her, soothingly.

Live fish could have swum in Billhook's stomach. He tried to see between the soldiers as they closed around the boat again. Was it them? Tama Hine? That little bundle? And Moennan? Were they alive? For a moment he closed his eyes and appealed to his mother. Mother, what have I done? Have I done right this time?

In swift, coordinated movements, the soldiers stepped away from the boat. They made two lines from the boat to the reedy dune, faced each other and placed out their arms to space themselves. They turned about until they were facing the strange crowd of exiles and countrymen at the garrison.

"Forward march," shouted the sergeant. There were other people, including the Major, behind them but Billhook could not see them for soldiers. They marched in two lines towards the garrison, past the white tents and the storehouse. When the first soldiers arrived within twenty steps of where the families, Billhook and Pigeon stood, they stopped suddenly.

Through the avenue walked the private who'd refused to flog the prisoner Ryan. He led Samuel Bailey, his hands cuffed in front of him. Bailey raised drink-ruined eyes to Billhook but gave little sign he knew him, a slight twitch at the corner of his mouth and that was all. He was shambling, taking small steps. Billhook realised that he wore leg irons. The soldier dragged him from the column of soldiers and took him to the storehouse.

Billhook expected cries of anger or outrage from the old women, or even a warrior stance from the young men. But they seemed disinterested in Bailey and were either entranced by the Major's theatre of British justice or, as Billhook was, more intent on seeing who came next.

The Major carried her. She cried out as he shifted her body in his arms. As they came closer, the kui woman shouted what sounded like a lament and then "Moennan!" Her young countrymen began to weep first, tears streaming down their faces, their hands making graceless, angry gestures. The face of the older man, possibly her husband, hardened, his jaw clenched. The Major put her down and stepped back. A shocked hush fell over the entire congregation as they saw what Samuel Bailey had done.

Ae, my mother, my mother, you are right. I am one of them. All I wanted was the woman … and I delivered her to this.

She stood alone with the crowd of people circled around her. Her hair was matted, not with dirt or salt, but blood. One eye was swollen shut. Moennan's legs were covered in grazes. The deeper cuts looked like knife wounds. Some wounds were festering. She held her left arm against her cloak as though it were broken.

The old woman was the first to move, helped by her sisters to stand before Moennan. She wept as she gently touched Moennan's face with her big hands. She spoke to her quickly and softly and Moennan too began to cry. Gradually others came to her side, even the boys who were at first too awed by the sight of her to come near.

Billhook stood well away, held his hand to his mouth.

The Major, who had flogged a man only days before, whispered to the surgeon, "Never before have I seen a person so ill-used by another."

Small fingers tugged at Billhook's. He looked down.

Hine. Tama Hine.

"Ae, Hine!" He went to grasp the child, to swing her up and into his arms but felt her flinch away just before he touched her waist and so he tugged back at her fingers instead.

"Tama Hine, my child. Hine."

He squatted down to see her proper. Around her neck lay

the gleaming string of shells that Dancer had made for her. She looked uncertainly at Billhook and grasped his hand tighter.

"Did he hurt you? Are you hurt, Tama Hine?"

She still wore the bloodied pants of the drowned American boy and her fur cloak. Her hair had grown, *she* had grown, since he last saw her sailing out through the inlet mouth with Bailey and Jimmy the Nail. She nodded and her lips trembled before they squared and tears leaked silently from her closed eyes.

For several minutes the young Māori and the child stayed where they were, holding hands, eyes closed and weeping soundless tears. He could never make it right again. Not ever, not since the moment he saw Bailey rushing through the scrub with her wriggling under one arm. His tears were not for the child but his knowing what he had done, enough that she stood here now and told him that she was hurt. Leaving his home Otakau on a grand mission of vengeance, to right a man's wrong that happened years before and here he was helping the wrong man along. As he was happy to see Tama Hine alive, he also felt broken with shame and could not muster the anger he needed to rebuild himself again.

The Lieutenant's man who had carried her ashore stepped between them. "I'll take her to her family now, Mr Hook."

"No."

"They are waiting for her," the ensign pointed to Moennan's family who were clustered about her. They were still sobbing and one of the old women wailed in what sounded like one of Billhook's family laments. A funereal, yet strangely celebratory, wailing.

"No. That is not her family."

"Mr Hook, it is not for you to instruct me."

Billhook released the child and smiled at her through bleary eyes. The ensign took her hand and led her over to the tight, noisy knot of Moennan's family. The Major and the surgeon went with him and together, the three men presented Tama Hine to them.

The wailing stopped as they considered the child. The old women looked at her curiously. The young men had seen her with the sealers before. They muttered to the old women. She belonged with the sealers.

"Hine! Tama Hine!" said Moennan. She spoke to the young men in language and then looked beyond them. She saw Billhook.

He could see, despite her broken face and closed eye, the same look she'd given him when she'd been surprised in the forest clearing. Startled, defiant, beautiful, but now something new, a knowing coolness. He shivered with that cool glance and then flushed hot.

Moennan nodded to Billhook and he nodded back. But she was indicating him to her family, not greeting him. She spoke to them and nodded his way again. One of the older men spoke in language to the Major, shaking his head at Hine and pointing to Billhook. The Major, in a moment of bewilderment, called on Pigeon to translate. Pigeon, although he knew no local language, was happy to make himself useful in a transaction that seemed quite obvious to everyone.

"The child, she not with these people, Boss. They say Billhook. Billhook looks after her."

The surgeon gave a blanket to Moennan. She sniffed at it warily and offered it to the old woman. He began to inspect her wounds, applying salve and bandages. She shrieked when he touched her broken arm. He spoke to her gently as he treated her. Finally, with Moennan trussed in white bandages around her head and her arm, the surgeon handed the old woman a small calico bag of ship's biscuit and indicated that they were for Moennan.

There was an odd, formal moment, spoken in two languages from opposite ends of the world, between the surgeon, the Major and Moennan's family. When they had finished talking Moennan left the garrison, one of the older men walking close and guarded beside her as though in a marriage ceremony, the old women and children following behind them. They stepped through the reeds and purple flowers, around a perfectly round granite boulder, and into the red gum forest where the sea eagles nested. Billhook saw a flash of her stark, white bandages, and then he never saw her again.

King George Sound 1827

The Māori left on the ship with the little girl and Moennan did not see Wiremu Heke nor Tama Hine again. Six moons later she birthed a child, a fine, strong boy and she named him after the surgeon who had cared for her when she returned from the island. The surgeon continued to give extra food to her and her boy, and he was the only white man the other women would talk to, for a long time.

It was good that Bailey and Heke and even Hine were gone, for they brought only chaos with them, and no law. But she still thought of them. When she remembered those terrible days on the island and the fear and the shame, she made a picture of the inlet again. That night on the water, when she was the tallest, moving that boat across the water with her big stick. How powerful she was. How quiet they were. Only the drips falling from her stick into a sea flashing with light and colour. And Wiremu Heke whispering to the child, "Fire in the water, Tama Hine. There. Hine. There. Fire in the water."

The *Amity* brig, February 4ᵗʰ–20ᵗʰ 1827

The brig is a pig. The brig is a pig, was Bailey's song as the *Amity* rolled with a following wind, sloughing and wallowing into the troughs. *She's a nasty little pig, this shit of a brig.* His hands grasped at me whenever I passed the crate he was locked within. At night, as we tried to sleep in the swinging hammocks under deck and Tama Hine shut her eyes tight and pretended to sleep, I heard him singing his grievous, shambling versions of a sea shanty. *Give me truth and give me clemency, Darky Hook, for I did not shoot the blackfella.*

I knew Bailey's crimes and I wanted him to swing. I wanted to drive a splicing pike through one of his eyes and throw his body to the monsters that dogged our wake. But there was just one man to be tried for murder upon this ship borne east and it was not to be me.

"Where, Wiremu? Where we go?" Tama Hine asked me as we stood at the bow, sailing through the heads of Princess Royal Harbour and into the Sound. She scratched at her new clothes. Before we left, the surgeon had taken her fur cloak and her trousers and thrown them on a fire, shaking his head at the bloodstains. He dressed her in a sackcloth frock and a cap made of spun wool.

We passed between Breaksea and Michaelmas, the channel ringing with barking dogs on the island.

"Who will look after Splinter?" Hine asked.

I told her that the lurcher would feast on fish and berries and birds, and grow fat and old on the island with his friends. "We go to Sydney town, Tama Hine. Long way."

"Can I go home, Wiremu?" She knew her way home, that sprite, for she had travelled these waters several times now.

"I will talk to the Lieutenant," I told her. It was all I could do, for our lives no longer belonged to us but were mapped by the Major's scrawls upon sheafs of paper.

The child is to be taken to Sydney on the Amity *for the disposal of the Governor.*

I was to testify to the sergeant there, the Major had told me. I was to tell the lawman the story of the Green Island killing and that the prisoner Samuel Bailey did this crime. My statement was locked in Lieutenant Festing's safe, to be presented in Sydney. "There is no recourse to law here yet," the Major told me. "Samuel Bailey is not a convict but a free man and not subject to arbitrary punishment. He must go to Sydney to face British justice."

I do not understand the white man's law. I do not understand why they must send the child away to the other side of her world. I do not understand why Pigeon, Jimmy the Nail and Smidmore were accepted into the fledgling settlement and given rations for their skills alone, for they too had done terrible things, and why Tama Hine must leave. Mary and Dancer came in from the island with Tommy North and Neddy and were given rations too. The islanders were shunned by the soldiers, who held no power over them, and by the convicts for the same reason. Smidmore, Everett and Pigeon, even the Vandiemonian Worthies, they treated the land people with contempt. They carried their own mana, for they had seen things that land people never saw. And yet Hine had to leave.

"We are close now, Wiremu," said Hine after three days at sea, and sure enough the Doubtful Islands appeared on the horizon:

misty, grey mounds squatting in the sea just off the red cliffs.

I spoke to the ship's captain, Hansen. He squinted at the hazed horizon and called over the Lieutenant.

"Mr Hook is requesting that we take the child back to her people who live near here, sir. But we shall soon have to beat out to sea by the looks of those clouds."

"Then let's beat out," said Festing. "The Major's instructions are that I take the child to Sydney."

The Lieutenant would not move from his orders. Tama Hine sat with me on the bridge and we watched her country slide away. The hazy clouds on the horizon brought on the weather and the captain screamed to the men on the spars as he turned the ship into the wind. "Harden them up, yer bastards. Harden up!"

*

Three days and three nights with no sight of land. Tama Hine pretended to sleep in her hammock and when I looked over during Bailey's fruity ramblings, she quickly shut her eyes. Bailey stayed in his cramped little cage and every morning a ship's mate took away his bedpan that had lain pitching and stinking all the night. The hold smelled of vomit and the leftover scents of animals and people from its last voyage.

The Lieutenant ordered the captain to bring the ship in close to Israelite Bay, to rescue Jack and Tommy. It was nearly a year since they were abandoned there by our Boss Davidson. We lowered a little boat into the sea. The Lieutenant, two of the mates and I rowed towards the blinding white shores of the cove. We circled the island, part of what the Lieutenant called The Eastern Group, searching the sky for smoke and the craggy, stone edges of the island for people or huts, but saw nothing, only clouds of terns rising from the island.

The boat grunted onto the rocks. We climbed out and waded

through the water. "Up here," I told the Lieutenant. "This is where Boss told them to camp." Over the reddening succulents and the reeds and into the grove of peppermints, we found the hut made from bent saplings and branches. It was cool and green in the forest and vines grew through the hut and over its doorway. Jack and Tommy had not been there for a long time.

"Their water cask is not here," I said to the Lieutenant.

The men threw half a dozen rolled and salted sealskins into the boat. We took the short journey to the beach and split up to search for the brothers. It is a lonely thing to search for men, to not know where to look and what you may find. The Lieutenant and I walked along the shore to the western end of the beach. Neither of us spoke but listened instead to the squeaks of our feet in the sand.

We climbed the rocks sprinkled in shattered turban shells, to a tiny bay gleaming white as the one before but broken in half by a freshwater stream. The Lieutenant saw the cask before I did.

"They must have gone for water," he said, hurrying along the beach.

The twins lay on the sand above the high tide mark on the other side of the creek. Their bodies were dried to leather and bone and their shredded clothes flapped in the light wind. Eyeless sockets opened to the sky. Jack's tattoo of the upended *Governor Brisbane* was touching his brother's arm and they clasped sinewed, fleshless hands.

The Lieutenant knelt beside the bodies. Tiny black ants scurried around his knees. I roved my eyes over the bush that surrounded us, breathing in the sweat of the trees in the midday heat, listening.

"Death spear, this one," said the Lieutenant. He'd pulled aside the rags of Tommy's shirt to show the jagged hole in his breast. "The barb is lined with tiny pieces of knapped quartz. Look. The quartz falls off like shark's teeth. Push the spear in and out a few times and death comes as fast to a man as cutting his throat. Cuts every artery. But this one," he moved to Jack's body. "This one …" He peeled away more cloth. "I cannot find a mark on him." He rolled Jack's body towards his brother's. Maggots spilled away onto the sand. "There is no way of knowing."

"Jack was not a man to lay down and die." I touched their clasped hands. Where Tommy's fingers were open and straight, Jack had gripped his brother's hand tight before he died.

The two other men found our sorry party and we buried Jack and Tommy where they lay. We used the oars as shovels. Jack's hand could not be prised from his brother's and so they were buried that way. The Lieutenant sacrificed an oar to the double grave, driving it deep into the sand so that it stood as a marker, "like a sapling", as Boss Davidson had said all that time ago. One of the ship's mates said a brief prayer. We carried the oars along the lonely beach, climbed into the boat and rowed back to the ship.

*

The rest of the journey to Sydney was slow and we waited out a stilling of the wind in Bass Strait for days. At night I lay with my flesh rolling over my bones in the gentle sway of the brig. I did not sleep often, for Bailey did not sleep. I knew the man could go for days without shutting his eyes and that he dreamed more when he was awake. During the nights Bailey pestered me with his stories of Elizabeth.

"That child Elizabeth," he croaked from inside his crate one night. "She was mine too, you know. It wasn't only father who had her. She was always a whore. I went back for her later. Before father was done for embezzlement we had a fine time, my father and I. No wonder mother died from the melancholy. She had no money left for the high life and then it was just father and I and Elizabeth."

"Be quiet, Bailey."

People have always told me things. Bailey seemed to warm to telling me his scourge of a life, wanted to confess and was not quiet. He took pleasure in telling me the black children he'd had in Van Diemen's Land. Other things I shall never say aloud for fear of rotting my own tongue in my mouth. I was filthied by his stories. I would have asked for the night watch but then Tama Hine would be alone with him.

"What will happen to the child, Captain?"

"Ahh, you are a New Zealand native then, Mr Hook!"

The ship's master, Hansen, was a doughty, bluff man in his sixties with a neck that fell in two giblets. He was drinking whisky in the companion way and willing to talk. Always been a seaman, he said, although he tried farming once, sold the land and went back to being master.

"My most pleasant memory is the service we held on Christmas day for the Māori." He told me, most prideful, that he was a close associate of the chief chaplain, Reverend Marsden, and that together they had set up the first English settlement in New Zealand. I searched my mind for the name Marsden and it was the whaler at Doubtful Island Bay, John te Marama from Rangihoua Pā, who had lived with the Reverend.

"My daughter Hannah is married to one of his missionaries, see ... though there was a spot of trouble for a while there with my wife regarding muskets. That wife of mine never did give up meddling when it comes to trade and helping our daughter and son-in-law. Never 'til the day she died. God rest her soul. Gun-runner and drunkard, the Reverend said. Giving the natives muskets made for a lot of trouble between them and the missionaries, he said ... ahh well ... perhaps Marsden and I aren't such close associates anymore. He shouldn't have said that about my wife. He was wrong. Dead wrong."

"Where will the child go?" I asked again.

"What child?" The master was lost to his memories. "Oh, the native kid. I'll take her to William Hall. A good man, a good man. He's in charge of the Native Institution at Parramatta now. Knew him well from the Rangihoua mission. One of Marsden's men. Good man. Fanny Bailey will be Christianised. Christianised, Mr Hook."

Fanny Bailey.

I left Hansen to his drink. My thoughts jammed upon that name. Fanny Bailey. I knew that Lockyer had called her Fanny after a child of his own. But her name was not Fanny Bailey. Her name was … Hine. To me. Tama Hine. And to her now. That she was named after Samuel Bailey made my stomach lurch. Her name, scratched out on paper by the white man. She would hear his name called aloud every day at the Native Institution. Her name *was not* Fanny Bailey.

My sick feeling led me to the stern to stare at an idling, flattened wake. My mind cleared. It was as we were becalmed in Bass Strait, that I decided what I must do when we arrived in Sydney.

Every night I distracted Hine from Bailey's night ranting and mutterings, teaching her my language. The ship's timbers creaked and shackles clanked against the masts. I squatted against the planks and Tama Hine sat on a pile of rope facing me.

"Ko Tama Hine toku ingoa means 'my name is Tama Hine'," I said. "What is your name?"

"Ko Tama Hine toku ingoa," she said.

"What is your name? Say it again, Hine."

"Ko Tama Hine toku ingoa."

"Ae, you are clever, Tama Hine."

She nodded to me and looked nervously to Samuel Bailey's cage.

"Yes," I nodded. "Ae."

She nodded again. "Ae."

"No," I shook my head. "Kahore, or kao."

She shook her head too. "Kahore."

"I am hungry. Kei te hiakai ahau. I am hungry."

"Kei te hiakai ahau," she said.

"I am full, not hungry. Kei te kī ahau. Kei te kī toku puku. I am full. I am not hungry. I come from Doubtful Island, from west coast of Port Jackson Land." Because I knew that when asked, Tama Hine could not say where she came from. As a seven year old, her country was the centre of her world and did not need a name. But if ever she wanted to find her way home without me, she needed to name it.

"I come from Doubtful Island, from west coast of Port Jackson Land. Say this now Tama Hine: 'No Doubtful Island ahau, kī te Tai Hau-a-uru o Poihakena.' Say where your home is, Hine."

"No Doubtful Island –" she faltered.

"– ahau, kī te Tai Hau-a-uru o Poihakena," I prompted.

"No Doubtful Island ahau, kī te Tai Hau-a-uru o Poihakena. My home is Doubtful Island."

Sydney February 20th 1827

"In your statement, William Hook, you say that the prisoner shot dead the man on Green Island." The sergeant became angry and shoved a scrunched paper at me.

The air was silky and hot in Sydney town and the place where I sat with the sergeant was thick with heat and flies. I heard the music of a metal cup bouncing on stone in the next room.

"I did not say Samuel Bailey shot the black man. I said Samuel Bailey was in the boat when the black man was shot."

The sergeant straightened the paper on his rough table, held it at arm's length and read again.

"I am telling you the truth, sir," I said.

He shook his head and I became afraid that I would not make it back to the docks and to Tama Hine before she was taken.

"But Major Lockyer states clearly in his letter to the Colonial Secretary that Samuel Bailey ..." he wiped his freckled hand through his hair. "Mr Hook, can you read English?"

"No sir."

"In your statement to the Major, you say that Samuel Bailey was in the boat but nothing of Samuel Bailey killing the man. And yet the Major wanted him charged with murder. This puzzles me." He threw my statement onto the table and I stared at the strange marks sloping across the page. "I shall keep the prisoner here until I hear otherwise. You are free to go."

I ran to the docks. I ran through streets paved in wood and stone and past the horses, dodged the people who sold or begged food from their hands, past the gangs of men heaving adzes into the ground and the clanging of metal against stone. At the docks I ran towards the twin masts of the *Amity* and a cart waiting alongside, the horse champing into a nosebag, resting one leg. Straight up the gangplank and down the hatch to where Tama Hine swung in her hammock. The glee that spread across her face crept away when she saw my panic.

"Where is Hansen? Where is the Lieutenant?"

"They talking, Wiremu. In their cabin," she whispered and pointed aft.

"Do you have your things, if we go now?"

Tama Hine pretended to busy herself looking around the hold for a sack of her belongings. She pulled a piece of pumice stone from under her frock and grinned at me. "This."

*

For seven days we lived like ghosts on the docks, sleeping during the day in places nobody could find us. At night I went to the bars where men and women swung out of the doors and the place heaved with music and the people swayed and sang together like one great monster of the deep. I cut the child's hair short with a knife so that she looked like a ship's boy and taught her more of my countryman's language.

Maybe one day Tama Hine will decide to journey to her home country. For now I taught her to be strong, to protect herself and to ready herself for when that day comes.

On the seventh day, the same day a storm stood like a grey wall out to sea, Tama Hine and I found a berth on a whaler bound for my southern island Otakau.

"In times of trouble," I said to the child as we sailed through the heads of Sydney Harbour towards the storm, "be strong! Be brave! Be of big heart, Hine!"

And as the rain smacked into the sails, Tama Hine shouted back to me: "Āhākua nga uaua, kia kaha! Kia toa! Kia manawanui, Wiremu Heke!"

And so we were going back to my home, together. I did not know what awaited us there. Maybe Te Rauparaha had already cut his way through our village. I did not know. I did not know. I did not know anything of James Kelly. I had given up on that vengeance long ago.

Author's Note

The Sound is based on a true story of the men, women and children who travelled from Bass Strait to King George Sound in 1825–1826 on the sealing schooners *Hunter* and *Governor Brisbane*. To get an idea of the lives of the Breaksea Islanders, you can find their individual biographies and a historical rendition of events at my website **www.sarahdrummond.org**

Relics, Curiosities and Autographs

On being swallowed by a whale

The Star of the East was in the vicinity of the Falkland Islands and the lookout sighted a large Sperm Whale three miles away. Two boats were launched and in a short time one of the harpooners was enabled to spear the fish. The second boat attacked the whale but was upset by the lash of its tail and the men thrown into the sea, one man being drowned, and another, James Bartley, having disappeared, could not be found. The whale was killed and in a few hours was lying by the ship's side and the crew were busy with axes and spades removing the blubber. Next morning they attached some tackle to the stomach which was hoisted on the deck. The sailors were startled by something in it which gave spasmodic signs of life, and inside was found the missing sailor doubled up and unconscious. He was laid on the deck and treated to a bath of sea water, which soon revived him ... He remained two weeks a raving lunatic ... At the end of the third week, he had entirely recovered from the shock and resumed his duties.

– John Wilson Ambrose, "The Sign of the Prophet Jonah and its Modern Confirmation", *Princetown Theological Review*, vol. 25, 1927. In Heathcoate Williams, *Whale Nation*, Harmony Books, New York, no date, p. 165.

The War of the Worlds

The inspiration for *The War of the Worlds* came one day when Wells and his brother Frank were strolling through the peaceful countryside in Surrey, south of London. They were discussing the invasion of the Australian island of Tasmania in the early 1800s by European settlers, who hunted down and killed most of the primitive people who lived there. To emphasise the reaction of these people, Frank said, "Suppose some beings from another planet were to drop out of the sky suddenly and begin taking over Surrey and then all of England!"

– Malvina G. Vogel, Foreword to H. G. Wells, *The War of the Worlds*, Great Illustrated Classics, Abdo Publishing Company, 2005.

The spear in the seal in the shark in the sand

Several seals were procured on this and the preceding day, and some fish were caught alongside the ship; but our success was much impeded by three monstrous sharks, in whose presence no other fish dared to appear. After some attempts we succeeded in taking one of them; but to get it on board required as much preparation as for hoisting in the launch. The length of it however was no more than twelve feet three inches but the circumference of the body was eight feet. Amongst the vast quantity of substances contained in the stomach, was a tolerably large seal, bitten in two, and swallowed with half of the spear sticking in it with which it had probably been killed by the natives. The stench of this ravenous monster was great, even before it was dead; and when the stomach was opened it, it became intolerable.

– Matthew Flinders, the *Investigator*, January 12th 1802.

On disabling a navy in 1817

… as we were unable to leave owing to the wind being dead against us. Early next morning there was a great crowd on the beach making a great noise of lamentation over the death of their chief. Closely watching their movements, we concluded that they were about to launch their canoes and make another attack upon us, and we deemed it advisable to prevent them doing so, if we could. Accordingly we immediately manned our two boats, taking arms and ammunition with us, and pulled close to where the canoes were lying, determined if possible to destroy them at once. As the boats neared the shore the Natives made back into the bush. One of the boat's crew landed: the other kept afloat, to cover the men on shore with their muskets. With three long cross-cut saws the whole navy was speedily disabled. On seeing the havoc that was being made of their canoes, some of the more daring of the Natives ventured out of their cover and made a rush at our men, but a well-directed volley levelled several of their number, and terrified the rest so that they again took to the bush.

Both sides are now highly excited and bent on revenge.

– Unknown informer, 1817, Frank Tod, "The *Sophia* Affair", in *Whaling in Southern Waters*, Dunedin City Council, Dunedin, 1986, p. 138.

Dear Mr Kelly

21 May 1833
Otago, New Zealand.

To Mr James Kelly.

Sir,

This to certify that the Natives of Otago have threatened to take your ship from Capt. Lovett, stating that you had formally (sic) killed or wounded several years ago some of their people and that they would have revenge. Most of the people also deserted the vessel at the above Port.

I have the honour to be,

Your obedient Servt.

J. B. Weller

– Frank Tod, "The *Sophia* Affair", in *Whaling in Southern Waters*, Dunedin City Council, Dunedin, 1986, p. 139.

Mr Thistle's doomsayer

This evening, Mr Fowler told me a circumstance which I thought extraordinary; and afterwards it proved to be more so. Whilst we were lying at Spithead, Mr Thistle was one day waiting on shore, and having nothing else to do he went to see a certain old man named Pine, to have his fortune told. The cunning man informed him that he was going out on a long voyage, and that the ship, on arriving at her destination, would be joined by another vessel. That such was intended he might have learned privately; but he added, that Mr Thistle would be lost before the other vessel joined. As to the manner of his loss, the magician refused to give any information. My boat's crew, hearing what Mr Thistle said went along also to consult the wise man and after the prefatory information of a long voyage, were told that they would be shipwrecked but not in the ship they were going out in: whether they would escape and return to England, he was not permitted to reveal.

This tale Mr Thistle had often told at the mess table; and I remarked with some pain in a future part of the voyage, that every time my boat's crew went to embark with me in the *Lady Nelson,* there was some degree of apprehension amongst them that the time of the predicted shipwreck had arrived. I make no comment upon this story but recommend a commander if possible to prevent any of his crew from consulting fortune tellers.

– Matthew Flinders, the *Investigator*, February 22nd 1802. (Mr Thistle had drowned the previous evening.)

Cave sealing

The other youngster and I stayed on the bridge to drag out the seals from the two inside. They kindled a light, and when they reached the end of the cave, there was a beach full of seals there – big and little, male and female. *Bainirseach* is the name of the female seal, and the male is called the bull. There are some of them that it's absolutely impossible to kill.

– Tomas O'Crohan, *The Islandman,* Oxford University Press, Oxford (1937), 2000, p. 99.

Heterotopia of the boat

Brothels and colonies are two extreme forms of heterotopia, and if we think, after all, that the boat is a floating piece of space, a place without a place, that exists by itself, that is closed in on itself and at the same time is given over to the infinity of the sea and that, from port to port, from tack to tack, from brothel to brothel, it goes as far as the colonies in search of the most precious treasures they conceal in their gardens, you will understand why the boat has not only been for our civilisation, from the sixteenth century until the present, the great instrument of economic development (I have not been speaking of that today), but has also been simultaneously the greatest reserve of the imagination. The ship is the heterotopia par excellence. In civilisations without boats, dreams dry up, espionage takes the place of adventure, and the police take the place of pirates.

– Michel Foucault, "Of Other Spaces", *Diacritics* vol. 16. no. 1, Spring 1986, pp. 22–27.

Romancing the Sound

Night	Kartiac
Day	Ben, bennan
Star	Chindy
Moon	Meuc
Sun	Chaat
Thunder	Condernore
Lightning	Yerdivernan
Morning	Mania
Tomorrow	Maniana
Yesterday	Kartiac kain
By and by	Poordel
Just now	Yibbel
Some time since	Corram
Long time since	Corram quatchet
Evening	Corramellon
Cold	Mulgan
Hot or warm weather	Ureler
Young	Eeniung, tooting
Sleep	Copil
Sleep together	Copil nahluc
Listen	Yuccan

– Surgeon Nind, King George Sound, 1827.

Moennan and Manilyan

Wanting to know the ideas of the blacks of the origin of mankind, I got him [Mokare] this evening after some difficulty to understand my questions, when he told me that a very long time ago the only person living was an old woman named Arregain who had a beard as large as the garden. She was delivered of a daughter & then died. The daughter called Moenang grew up in course of time to be a woman, when she had several children, (boys & girls), who were the fathers and mothers of all the black people.

[Mokare] [t]old me this evening that Moken had commenced, which he knew by the situation of the Black Magellanic cloud near the cross (Whitepepoy). They have some story which I could not clearly make out, of its being an emu and laying eggs. The larger White Magellanic cloud he called the Chucadark & mentioned the names of several stars. One brilliant one was shortly to be seen, called Manilyen.

– Collet Barker, in John Mulvaney and Neville Green, *Commandant of Solitude. The Journals of Captain Collet Barker 1828–1831*, Melbourne University Press, 1992, p. 289.

Splinter, King of Breaksea Island

I should mention that on Breaksea Island, there are a vast number of European dogs, evidently the produce of animals left there, by ships passing. How they managed to subsist themselves, it is difficult to conceive, but there they certainly are, and if a ship in coasting along the shore, fires a shotted gun at the rocks, she will be speedily answered by the loudest barking.

– Colonel Hansen, *The Perth Gazette and Western Australian Journal*, January 26th 1833.

ACKNOWLEDGEMENTS

It takes many more people than an author to create a book. Firstly my most heartfelt thanks go to two amazing women who have been my bedrock over the last five years: Kathryn Trees and my mum Carmelita O'Sullivan. I'd also like to thank my dad John Drummond and my children, Maya Pearl Drummond and Morgan Lindberg.

For ideas, inspiration and friendship: Bob Howard, Michelle Frantom, Murray Arnold, Carol Petterson, Lynette Knapp, Chris Pash, Vernice Gilles, Penny Bird, Lester Coyne, Harley Coyne, Jon Doust, Simon Smale, Tuaari Kuiti, Yann Toussaint, Alex Levak, Ron Fewster, Sheilah Ryan and Paul Ireland, Colin Ryan, Selina Hill and Jay Cook, Karen Atkinson, Kim Scott, Jim Everett, Patsy Cameron, Tarquin Smart, Tim and Justine Gamblin, Aileen Walsh, Julie Gough, Dan Cerchi, Malcolm Traill, Ciaran Lynch, Melissa Collins, Adam Wolfe and Bill North.

Colin and Holly Story, staff at the UWA Albany campus and Mike Murphy have given me quiet, beautiful places to write. The support and guidance of the Fremantle Press team is incredible and in particular I'd like to acknowledge Georgia Richter's intuitive editorial input into the manuscript that became *The Sound*.

ABOUT THE AUTHOR

Sarah Drummond lives on the south coast of Western Australia. She is the author of *Salt Story: of sea-dogs and fisherwomen,* a memoir and social history of commercial estuarine fishers. In 2014, *Salt Story* was longlisted for the Dobbie Literary Award and shortlisted for the Western Australian Premier's Book Awards. *The Sound* is her first novel.

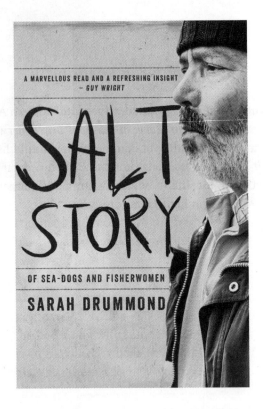